Never Been Called Pretty
A Short Story Collection

NEVER BEEN CALLED PRETTY

A SHORT STORY COLLECTION
BY AUTHOR ZEE. W

www.zbookpublishing.com

ZBook Publishing, LLC
P.O. Box 2085
Stone Mountain, GA 30087
www.zbookpublishing.com

Never Been Called Pretty
First Edition
ZBook Publishing, LLC

ISBN- 978-1-941689-03-5

Dedication

This book is dedicated to everyone who's had the strength to overcome a traumatic situation and evolve.

-Author Zee.W

PLEASE GET HELP

If you or someone you know is a victim of domestic violence
or sexual abuse, please get help.

Domestic Abuse Hotline: 1-800-799-SAFE (7233)
Sexual Abuse Hotline: 800.656.HOPE (4673)

Contents

Where The Eagles Don't Fly

I T WASN'T HARD for Jerica to convince Charles to meet her at an abandoned warehouse almost an hour away from his home. He felt that he owed it to her. He needed to see her. He needed her to accept his apology. This was his only chance. So, when the phone rang late in the night, he kissed his wife and children and told them him he would be back. Little did he know, Jerica had different plans.

Charles' body was stuffed in the corner of a wall. Jerica managed to catch him off guard, hitting him in the back of the head with the butt of her pistol. When he came to, he was tied up. He couldn't move. His long legs were bent and embedded deep in his chest. His shoes lodged underneath a thick book. His bottom lip trembled, dripping saliva onto his khaki pants. His white collared shirt was shredded and saturated with blood; pieces of flesh hung out of the slits. It looked as if he had been attacked by a lion. The metal frames of his eye glasses were bent and slid down the wide bridge of his sweaty nose. His eyes were wide and full of terror. He extended his arms and stretched his fingers out in a *stop* gesture. He tried to protect his face but the black leather whip always found its way to his flesh, shredding it from the muscle and ripping it from his bones. His loud cries were converted to faint

1

childlike shrieks as his constant screaming dried his voice out. With every strike, his energy depleted.

"You're right…you're right," his voice cracked. "Jerica just calm down and we can work through this," he patted the air with his hands. But Jerica had no mercy for him. She raised her arm and slashed his hands with the whip with such force sweat popped from her forehead and plopped on to his face. "Ahhh!" he cried out. His hands dripped with blood. Attempting to control his pain, he bit down on his bottom lip. His body trembled all over. He mouthed a silent prayer to himself. He knew she was going to kill him. There was no convincing her otherwise. And he also knew that Jerica would make sure his death was slow and painful.

"I am calm. More calm than I've been in a while," Jerica said back to him. Her voice showed no emotion. She looked down at his bleeding quivering body, staring blankly; she had no remorse. "You did this to me! It was you. You are my Doctor Frankenstein and I'm your monster. I'm the world's monster."

"No. I'm the monster," he said.

"Shut up," she lashed at him again. "Don't tell me who you are. I know who you are. Me and mamma. We both know. They don't know but we know. Now you say you pray every day. Pray!" she turned up her nose. "God actually listens to you?" Jerica twisted her face and shook her head, disgusted. "It aint right. You shouldn't be able to talk to God. Wrote that book talking bout you being saved well who's gone save me!" She screamed and lashed the whip across his face knocking off his glasses. "Who was there to save my mamma?" Jerica yelled and slashed the whip against various parts of his body like she was swatting at a fly. "That man should have never prayed for you. Nobody should have prayed for you. But they do. They all pray for you and care bout you but no one prays for me. No one."

"I pray." He pushed out the words through his bleeding, busted lips.

She raised her leg and kicked him, landing her foot forcefully onto his chest. "You think I want your prayer? You think I want anything from you other than your bleeding dying corpse? I loathe you Charles. I hate you so bad I taste it. I craved your death for years. I craved this moment and still it aint enough. Your death aint enough for me. My hate for you goes beyond the grave. I want to blow your brains out," she pulled a gun from the waist of her jeans and shoved it in his face. "I want to blow your brains out your head and stomp on the chunks. Smash them into this floor and smear them against the back of my shoe just like shit. I want to see your flesh pop and your skull crack into tiny pieces. I want to see your brain splatter across the room in small big chunks. I want to see you choke on the taste of your own blood. I want to hear you beg and beg for your life." She said all in one breath.

Jerica took a deep breath and exhaled blowing the air up towards the ceiling. The idea of Charles dying was exciting her too much.

"I am begging. I'm begging for my life now." He clasped his hands together and extended them towards her face.

"You aint begging. No…you aint begging, yet. You just trying to trick me like you tricked them. Trying to make me feel sorry for you like they do. The sorrow they give you is mine! You stole that from me just like you stole everything else. You can have my virginity that you stole. You can have my internal joy and happiness. Hell, you can even have my mamma because, for some reason, all she ever wanted was you but my sorrow you can't have!" she yelled. "That sorrow belongs to me. Those are my prayers they give you, it's my mercy God is showing to you. Mine and mine alone!" She wiped the sweat from her brow before placing the gun back in the waist of her pants.

"You gone have to beg. Beg me like the day I begged you. Remember? I said 'pleeeease don't kill my mamma. Pleeeease don't take her from me'. But you kept on choking her. You squeezed her skinny neck with your big gorilla hands until the spit foamed out her mouth like the dish soaps she used for my bubble baths; you squeezed her neck until her yellow complexion turned pink then blue; you squeezed my mamma's neck until her sad brown eyes rolled back into her head. Until they were nothing but red striped white balls! Then you let her go. Only cause you knew she wanted to die. You wouldn't give her life and you wouldn't give her death. You gave her just enough to cry, to

3

fear, to hurt. You fed off her fear. The self-mutilation she displayed by loving a man like you. And when you got bored with her you gave it to me. I wasn't like mamma though. At least I wasn't like her then. Then…" Jerica paused, "then I wanted to live.

"Mamma used to say I had potential to be strong like my real daddy, Alvin. She said it was in my blood and if there was one thing in the world she was going to teach me it was how to be strong. She used to say when Charles lay on top of you just close your eye real tight and think about Johnson Park. Mamma used to take me to Johnson Park when I was about three or four. It was before you. Before she got weak. It was when her brown eyes were so shiny they sparkled and her smile so big it showed her teeth and not her busted lips. She used to laugh so hard it made other people laugh.

"Her carefree spirit was contagious. She would take me to that park and push me on the swings. Back then, the air seemed so fresh and the grass, it was so soft and green." Jerica held her nose in the air as if she was inhaling the scent. "Mamma would push me so high in the air I could touch the clouds with the tip of my toes. Then she would say *'wanna go where the eagles don't fly?,'* and I would reply 'yes, Mamma, take me where the eagles don't fly' and she will count to one, and push, two, and push even harder, then say close your eyes, and by the time she counted to three I was flying where the eagles didn't," Jerica closed her eyes and extended her arms in a flying motion and circled around the room.

The memory caused a smile to stretch across her face. Then her eyes opened and the smile faded. "I loved being where the eagles didn't fly. Where happiness was made," Jerica said. "That's how she told me to be strong. She said when Charles is on top of you, just close your eyes and go where the eagles don't fly. I used to ask her is that where she be going when you use to be beating her. She say no. She say she couldn't go there no more. Then she seem real sad again. I didn't understand why then but I do now cause I can't go there no more either. I miss it," her voice trailed off. Jerica looked down at Charles. "But I got an idea of how to get back there," she said and pulled out the gun again, admiring what it was made to do before stuffing it back in the waist of her pants.

"Mamma taught me how to be strong the best way she could. I remember them folks from that church we use to sneak off to used to hug her and cry for her. She didn't care bout they pity though; she didn't need it. The pity she felt for herself was enough. She used to say to me, *'Jerica, they only pity me cause my bruises show on the outside.'* Then she would point to her black eye and red welted neck. *'But you,'* she would say, *'you darker than me',* she held out her high yellow arm and put it against my dark brown skin, *'your bruises only gone show on the inside. They gone be hidden from people to see but when you get ready, you show them your bruises cause people only gone care about what they can see, what's staring them right in the face. You reveal them bruises to the world when you get ready. You make people care'.* And that's exactly what I plan to do," Jerica said and kicked at Charles' bleeding body.

"My bruises still hidden though. Don't nobody see them. They may be able to see this one though," she pulled up her sleeve and extended her wrist revealing the thick welt of dead skin that scarred her wrist. "You can't steal this cause you didn't know bout it. I keep it hidden. I don't want nobody seeing my bruises," She traced the welt with her finger. "I did it just like mamma did. Same arm and everything," she continued to massage her wrist. "Mamma sat in that tub looking like she had been bathing in red beets. I always hated beets. The way they looked and smelled. Just like blood but that's what her blood looked like, red beets. I didn't know blood could get that thick and be so dark red it looked like black cherry. It floated on top of that cold water all the way up to her neck. Her body marinated in all that blood so long that her skin looked pasty and pale like the glue I used to play with in kindergarten. She still held the razor in her hand just in case she needed it in her afterlife. Her eyes stayed open though. I was surprised cause every time they show dead people on TV, their eyes be closed but not hers. They looked right at me. It looked like they were smiling at me. Then you came rushing in the room. You yanked her stiff body out that tub and threw her on the floor; cursing at her and punching her dead body. Like you could beat her back to life. But it was too late. She did what you didn't. She was in control and I was proud of her for it.

"I decided last year that I was gone be in control too. Just like mamma. I sat in a yellowed stained mildew ridden tub and slit my wrist and slit and slit until the blood poured out like a fountain. Now I know why mamma's eyes where smiling. It felt so good feeling my soul make its escape from my wretched body. Death feels better than life. I know that now. The blood oozed out my body so quick and heavy I felt faint. Then I felt like I was floating. Oh, I was so high in the sky just like when mamma used to push me on them swings. I was almost where the eagles don't fly, almost there. Seeing all that blood come out my lil ole wrist was amazing. It was like that blood held all my pain, all my sorrows; I was being set free. Then it stopped." She pulled her sleeve back down. "Guess God didn't want me like he wanted mamma. He didn't want me." Her eyes watered but she didn't cry.

"Maybe it's because he had a bigger purpose for you," Charles whispered.

"You're right," She said calm. "I think you're right Charles. Maybe my purpose is giving you back to the devil. Where you belong," She pushed the mouth of the gun against his forehead.

"No. Not anymore. I wrote the book to tell the world that people can change. Through God, people can change."

"But you, you revealed my bruises to the world and say they yours," She screamed in his face. "You a thief Charles. A low-down dirty thief." She leaned over and pulled out the book lodged under his feet. She held it in the air wearing a wicked smirk. She turned to the back and stared at his smiling picture. Then flipped back over to the front and read out, "Where The Eagles Don't Fly by Reverend Charles Willington." She spat on his face. "How dare you! You can't go there. You can never go where the eagles don't fly, never!"

"I know. I know. It's a dedication to your mother and yo…" She slapped him across the face with the book before he could finish. She spat blood onto his shoes and grimaced.

"I don't need you to tell my story! You hypocrite. You holy rolling hypocrite. This is what they love you for," she waved the book in his face. "*New York Times* number one best seller," she read the front cover.

"You got a wife now and two young daughters. How long before you start fucking them? How long does your precious wife have to live?"

"I'm a new man Jerica. God changed me. He changed me," Charles pleaded.

"Naw. Men like you don't got nothing new about them. You took my pain and turned it into yours and they gave you a best seller. A movie deal and TV interviews. And you got the nerve to get on TV talking bout 'thank God, I thank God for this', you need to thank me and my mamma. Putting our pain on display. Getting that book deal and movie deal. Enough money to build that mega church of yours that I plan to burn to the ground once I end you."

"Please don't do this. My church has programs that help men that were like me. I wrote the book to make the world better. To repent. To shout my sins from a mountain top."

Jerica took the whip and wrapped it around his neck and squeezed until he gasped for air.

"Your voice is the last voice I want to hear from a mountain top. A voice like yours ain't nothing but unnecessary noise and it needs to be silenced for good," she said then released him. His body slumped over as he sipped in slow bits of air in a bid to remain conscious.

"Showing my bruises and disguising them as yours to get money and sympathy is sick. And they listen to you. They say your change is remarkable," she read the reviews on the back of the book. "How could they look at you and see what they see? I don't understand. I don't care how many people you done prayed for or how many organizations you started for battered women and children. I don't care. You greedy, you just want those women and children pain too. You addicted to it!"

She flipped through the pages and stopped at a random page and read an excerpt. "I have lived on both sides of the world. I have been abused and was the abuser. I know the pain and was taught to give it. Possessing knowledge of this kind, I can stop it. Ha!" she yelled sarcastically. "You gone stop something you started? You can't stop that evil you spread," she dropped the book and pulled out the gun, poking it in his chest. "It done spread like wildfire. You can't stop me for sure.

Just like I couldn't stop you. Talking bout you training me. Always said that. *'Look, gal. I'm training you up on how to be a woman,"* She imitated his voice. *"Just lay there and be still. Don't say nothing'.* I never said nothing any way cause I was gone from there. I was where the eagles don't fly.

"You were my first life coach. After mamma died and they took me away, there was some more. Boy, what they did to me in them foster homes, woo," she sighed. "I guess it was a good thing you gave me some training cause I needed it. I sure did need it. By that time I was good at going where the eagles don't fly. I was so good them men thought it was something wrong with me. The way I would lay there stiff. No squirming, no crying. No begging them to stop; I was just paralyzed underneath and not just my lil ole 10-year-old body but my emotions too. They were paralyzed. It didn't stop them though. Man, they added to my training in such a way you would love to shake their hands. I should have gave you their names so you could thank them in the Acknowledgements of your dumb ass book. You would pat them on the back and say, *'good job fellows'.* All them foster homes and group homes. Same men, different faces.

"By the time I turned 13, I couldn't go no more. I just couldn't go where the eagles didn't fly. I don't know if my time expired or they locked me out cause they didn't want me no more. Maybe I was too tarnished. It had to be my group home counselor Randy that locked the doorway to where the eagles don't fly because after I met him, I was cast out.

"He wasn't like you. No, he didn't like me laying there looking dead underneath him. He hated it. He hated it so much he started doing all types of things to me to make me scream. Boy, that man flipped me over, tugged on me, bit me, pulled and scratched and pinched my insides with his rigid finger nails until I had to holla. I screamed and cried cause it hurt so bad. He liked that then. He was the first man to kiss me. Usually they aint like looking at my face. They would bury they faces in pillows or close their eyes while they were rocking on me but not Randy. Randy was one of a kind. I never forget the day he started biting and sucking on my lips. Ugh." Jerica closed her eyes and grimaced. "Then he stuffed that rum soaked, slim and tobacco-coated tongue of his in my mouth. I hated when he did that. Especially when he would smoke them stinking cigarettes. It was like he would smoke a pack of them nasty things then right after, push that nasty tongue in between my lips. To this day the smell of cigarette smoke turns my stomach so that I feel like I want to gag. Ugh," she held her stomach.

"He took where the eagles don't fly from me and you took my bruises. I'm gone pay him back though. Just like I'm paying you back. See, I don't forget nothing. You and him might pretend to forget but I don't. You know the saying that the student will outdo the teacher after a while, well that's like y'all too. Y'all taught me so well that I can outdo y'all. Y'all taught me how to kill and how to be killed. Y'all taught me how to spread hate instead of love and boy do I spread my hate. I spread my hate so far and so wide. Especially when I found out that my blood wasn't good no more. I mean I always knew I was no good but them doctors at that clinic made it more official. Talking bout if I don't accept treatment I'm gone die a slow and painful death. That was the best news I heard all year. Slow but sure, after a while God gone have to take me. But I aint leaving this world without leaving my mark. Disguising hate as love gets me in the door every time. Before I go, I'm gone try to kill all of you off.

"I spread hate to about 15 men so far. While they poking inside me with them death sticks, injecting me with the white and sticky evil, I'm injecting them with something too. I'm giving all my bad blood to them. All of it," she chuckled. "All the left over blood that was supposed to drain out of me the day I did this," she held up her scarred wrist, "it's all theirs now. All of it. I'm so good now, I got these fools paying me extra just to poke inside me with their death sticks without a condom. They be begging me to kill them and don't even know it," Jerica laughed.

Charles started to sob. He sniffed hard and lowered his head to the floor defeated. Jerica didn't pay his tears any attention.

"They push themselves inside this war hole I have between my legs without thinking they need a shield. They so stupid. Don't they know I'm like a one woman army in there? They too perverted to feel all the bruises I got up there. Pretty soon all y'all gone be gone and God gone pat me on the back. He gone place a crown on my head bigger than the size of heaven for all the good work I done."

Charles sniffed in air and held it for a few seconds before slowly pushing it out of his mouth. He looked up at Jerica and opened his mouth to say something but didn't. It was no use. He had created the monster that was craving his flesh. So, he continued to listen.

"Mamma gone be proud, too. She told me, '*Jerica you take out them bruises and show them to the world when you ready*'. I'm ready. I'm ready," She repeated, excited. "But first things first," she pulled back out the gun. "I got to rid the world of you."

Jerica spread her legs, standing her ground as she aimed the pistol at his mid-section. She smiled at him with evil eyes and perverse lips; she was ready.

"Lord, help her just like you helped me. I've done her so wrong, Lord, I've done her so wrong," he sobbed heavy.

"What you doing?" she kicked his feet. His prayers enraged her.

"Help her Lord, even after she takes me, help her. I see my sins in her. I see her pain, Lord, she's so hurt. She so hurt"

"Don't," she tried to cover her ears. "I don't want your prayer. I don't want your tears."

She pulled the trigger and stumbled back from the kick. Blood burst through his kneecap and Charles screamed out in pain.

"That's one," Jerica said calmly.

"She needs you Lord," Charles managed to say in between cries for help.

Jerica pulled the trigger again. This time, she didn't stumble. His second kneecap popped and a fountain of blood and bone flew out.

"That's two," Jerica said in an orgasmic tone.

Charles swallowed hard. He tried to curb the pain. "Lord please forgive me for…"

"Hell no," Jerica hit Charles in the mouth with the butt of the gun, knocking out his front teeth. "You get no forgiveness," she said.

She pointed the gun at his temple.

"I would say goodbye but I wouldn't mean it," she pulled the trigger and Charles fell over.

"That's three."

Jerica stared at Charles mutilated bleeding body. She looked at him long and hard and waited for her pleasure to come but it never came.

"I need to go back Lord. I need to go back to where the eagles don't fly. Please help me get there."

Jerica took a deep breath and stuffed the gun back in the waist of her pants. She kicked Charles' book across the room and spit on his dead body before slowly walking away.

The End

Ugly Girl

FAYE'S INSIDE GROANS were heavy but trailed out of her mouth like a faint whisper. She was good at controlling her pain. Not letting what she felt on the inside show on the outside. She followed her normal routine; take deep breaths in between punches and keep her eyes on a focal point so that she wouldn't pass out. It was similar to her jogging routine.

Usually, she could tell when he was about to retire. The punches became less forceful and the kicks got lighter. He would run out of creative words for insulting her and finally when he considered that he had done enough damage, when the blood was no longer neatly running down her face in organized streams but pouring in a messy spread that saturated her brows and dripped from her lips, he would stop. He would be so out of breath, he would fall against the wall using it as a crutch to support all 215 pounds of him. He would wipe the sweat from his brow and control his heavy breathing. Then, he would look down at the frail hunched over body that lay trembling under his feet. He would say, '*Go, get cleaned up*' in the most normal tone. Then she would clutch on to the closest table or chair and pull up what was left of her, scrapping her feet against the ground and shaking off the dizziness.

Sometimes, she would be so weak she would fall back down. He hated when she did that. He would grab her by her forearm and yank her up while yelling, '*Stop over reacting…damn…I hate when you do that,*' before pushing her in the direction of the bathroom.

This time was different though. It seemed that the punches never softened. Her focal point was blurred by blood and tears and although she was on the floor, with her bleeding nose buried against the ceramic tile, she felt like she was falling. She knew that she was about to pass out. It was funny; the things her mind ran on while he was beating her. The most trivial things. Nothing of major importance. Her grocery list, new accounts at her job or the last *Oprah* show she watched. Nothing relevant to what she was experiencing. It was her best way to deny what was happening. What her life had become under his hand. At least not until today.

Images of herself as a child flooded her mind. Even the stings from her skin popping and squirting blood as a result of his fist wasn't enough to keep the thoughts of her traumatic childhood away. The memory of her childhood was more painful than his kicks. Faye dreaded these memories.

FAYE SAT WITH her knees embedded on the soft shaggy rug. She was holding a picture of a light skinned black woman in her hand. Faye admired how the woman's straight silky hair hung down her shoulders. She admired the woman's narrow nose and thin lips that framed her oval shaped face. To Faye, women that looked like that were the most beautiful women she had ever seen. They were like angels. She prayed every day to wake up beautiful just like the women in the magazines. With scissors in her right hand, she eagerly flipped through the magazine cutting all the women out that she wished she looked like. This was something Faye made a habit of doing every night. It relaxed her mind and drowned out the negative insults that spewed from the mouths of the kids in her neighborhood. She had been called Ugly Girl for as long as she could comprehend words. But, looking

at the beautiful, almost impossibly perfect women that flourished on the glossy pages gave her hope. Sometimes Faye would tape the pictures on her forehead, covering her face, pretending to be the women. Other times, she would place a t-shirt on her head, covering her short kinks and pretend that she had long hair just like the women. She would flip the shirt across her shoulders and tie it up in a ponytail and imagine that she was light skinned with long hair. Faye knew that none of it was real, but it still made her feel beautiful.

Faye became obsessed with the women in the magazines. Their perfectly light skin looked clean and honest just like her sister, Rose. Everybody loved Rose. Her perfect complexion and curly long hair instantly made her a nice sweet girl. That's what everyone called Rose. A nice sweet girl. But Faye was Ugly girl. Grownups would look down at Rose and bask in her beauty but when they looked at Faye they either ignored her completely or gave her a sorrowful look.

So, Faye resorted to the magazine for comfort. Praying that one day, their beauty would fall on her. Whenever she saw a woman she liked, she carefully cut the image and put it in a neat stack. Sometimes she would only cut their features. Usually, hair or a nose or a smiling mouth with thin lips and shiny white teeth adorned with perfectly pink gums. When she was done, she would paste them to a piece of notebook paper and stick them in a folder. She put the folder under her pillow just like she did when she lost a tooth hoping that instead of sending the tooth fairy, God would send the beauty fairy to save her. Faye prayed that her dark complexion would be replaced with lighter skin, that her wide nose would slim down and that her tightly curled hair would loosen up and hang down her back, just like Rose and the women.

Looking through the magazines both excited and frustrated her. Excitement came from the fantasy that one day God would answer her prayer and she would wake up beautiful just like the women. The frustration came when she woke up in the same skin she had the previous morning. Sometimes she would analyze herself in the mirror. She would smile to see if God had started off by changing her teeth, but the reflection revealed back her dark gummed off white smile. "Shoot" she would say. Then she would pull the stocking cap from her head and hope that she would feel the soft, silky tresses she prayed would fall down onto her shoulder blades but this never happened either. She still kept her faith though. It was all she had.

"Faye Ann", she heard her grandmother call out. Faye quickly grabbed the magazine scraps and stuffed them in her folder. She didn't want her grandmother to see her cutting out the pictures. She knew that if she had, her grandmother would have a reason to insult her. She and her sister Rose where being raised by their grandmother. Their mother died of cancer when Faye was five and Rose was three. She knew that her grandmother liked Rose more than her because she was prettier. It was another reason she hoped that God would change her, then her grandmother would love her the same way she loved Rose.

"Coming, Grandma," She yelled.

"Don't come, get here," Her grandmother called back.

Faye was raised in a small town with small minded people. Where how you looked determined how far you would go in life. Who you would marry. What type of job you would get and how people treated you. The town's hobbies consisted of a stream of beauty pageants, local fashion shows, and debutante balls. These events were taken so seriously that the winners of the contests would be announced over the local radio station, their pictures would be printed in the paper, and the parents had a year's worth of bragging rights. People would greet the little girls in the stores and sometimes the managers even had their pictures hanging on the wall. The child winner instantly became the town's little celebrity. However, these shows were always typecast. All the girls always looked the same. Light skin and long hair. There was no escaping the mentality that Faye developed over the years. However, even with similar thinking, Faye knew she still didn't fit in with the rest of the town.

Faye walked into the country style kitchen with her head lowered to the vinyl floor. Her sister sat on a pillow in between her grandmother's legs while her grandmother stroked and brushed her long tresses. The neighbor was in the kitchen with her daughter too. Her daughter had the same long hair as Rose. Faye's grandmother and the neighbor gloated and gushed over how long their wards' hair had gotten and predicted how much longer their hair would be next year. It was their Saturday hobby. To sit and comb the girls' hair even though they weren't leaving the house. They treated them like living baby dolls. Faye's hair sat tangled and dry on top of her head, her grandmother never touched her hair. She would say that it was too short to style.

"Faye, clean them dishes and when you get done go outside to the neighbors and get my frying pot back."

"Can I go grandma?" Rose asked hopefully as she raised her head.

"No. That sun is shining too bright out there today. You don't want to get black like Faye. Do you?"

Rose lowered her head back down figuring her grandmother had a point. Even as a child, Rose knew that Faye was treated different because of how she looked. Rose felt blessed to be as pretty as she was.

"Erma, I just don't know where that girl came from," her grandmother said to the neighbor in a disappointed tone. She was referring to Faye. The neighbor sympathized with her grandmother as she shook her head in agreement.

"Her mother got fair skin and nice hair. I don't understand it either," Erma replied.

"That damn daddy of hers. I told that girl bout messing with the ugly black boys cross the tracks. Boy look like he just got off the boat. Skin blacker and crustier than my frying skillet. Faye got them strong African features. Wide nose, thick lips…" Her grandmother complained. "Just like her Daddy. They say his folks from somewhere in Africa."

"Yeah, but usually that light skinned gene is strong. I figured she would have some kind of color on her."

"Must have been God cursing her mamma for fooling around before she got married. She must have learned her lesson, thank God, cause Rose daddy more clear in complexion than me. See," her grandmother flipped her wrist and held up to Rose's cheek. "His people were mixed."

"Least she got the hair," Erma tried to give Faye some credit.

"Hm," she looked up at Faye and shook her head. "It won't grow past her ears. It's just a waste of texture." Her grandmother shook her head as she placed Rose's hair up into a high ponytail only to take it back down. Rose grimaced in agony. She didn't like being a human doll but still felt blessed.

"Good thing Faye smart cause she ain't gone ever get no husband looking the way she do. She gone have to take care of herself. But not my Rose," her grandmother leaned down and kissed Rose on the forehead. "She gone be able to have any man she want. She don't even have to finish high school. That's why I don't worry one bit about that bitter dark teacher she got. She always on top Rose talking about she need a math tutor. She just jealous. Rose gone marry up. You watch and see."

This was the type of conversations Faye had grown accustomed to inside her house. Outside the house, it was the same conversation but a different tune. The boys called her ugly and the girls called her blackie. She heard it so often from her grandmother, the neighbors, the people at the church that she had no choice but to believe it. Rose and the kids at school would call her ugly girl. She got so used to it that sometimes she would answer to it like it was her name and it wasn't long before she became the name, ugly girl.

FAYE'S SKIN BEGAN to burn from the brittle blades of the carpet. He was dragging her from the short hallway to the kitchen; she felt like she was floating. She wondered if she had died and was going up to heaven until she saw the back of his head through the slit of her swollen right eye. He had his thick hand clasped around her ankle. She could see traces of her blood on his knuckles. Faye felt worthless under his hand; like a worn out ragged doll being thrown out to the dogs. When he finally got to the kitchen, he slung her in between the corner of the dishwasher and the sink. Her face throbbed with pain and her breathing caused sharp stabs in her side. She prayed that he was finished. Her vision became more blurred and she started to feel her eyes grow puffier as the slits of her eyes got smaller and smaller. She heard the squeaking sound of him dragging her wooden chair across the ceramic tile. The noise stopped within distance of her.

The leather cushion of the chair whistled as he made himself comfortable. Faye couldn't see his face clearly but felt his evil glare; it intoxicated her with fear. He looked down at her body while fidgeting with a lighter. Faye heard the clicks of him trying to ignite the small flame. Her heart began to race at the idea of him watching her body burn alive. The same flesh she prayed for God to change all her life never felt more valuable. She remembered a time when she wanted to kill herself. The realization that she no longer wanted to live came to her like an epiphany; she wasn't expecting it. Faye wasn't expecting him either; he saved her. He brought her back to life, only to kill her again.

It was the day of her college graduation ceremony. She sat on her futon sofa and stared at her cap and gown. She had it neatly hung on her closet door with the hat attached to the top. It looked empty without a person in it, just like she felt. At this very moment she should have been walking across the stage, shaking the dean's hand as he handed her a golden plaque with her name embroidered on the surface. Not only had she graduated from one of the nation's top universities, she had done so with outstanding honors as her class' valedictorian. However, to Faye, this honor was better appreciated with love from family and friends.

Faye fantasized about this day. She imagined her grandmother going on and on about her granddaughter, being the only one minority out of the four percent of her graduating class to receive such great honors. Faye's grandmother loved to brag. She envisioned her grandmother placing a notice in the local newspaper and the church posting a 'congratulations' or 'we knew you could do it' announcement on the bulletin board. Faye remembered how thrilled her grandmother was when Rose won the teen beauty pageant. All the girls in the beauty pageant looked like Rose. In the end, it was the speech Faye wrote that won Rose the crown. Her grand-mother celebrated the victory as if she had been crowned herself, so surely she would celebrate a victory of this prestige with Faye. She would extend her arms to Faye and offer her years' worth of past due love; she would finally be proud to call Faye her granddaughter; she would finally realize that Faye too had a special gift different from Rose, but no one called. Not even to give a phony excuse as to why they couldn't make it.

The phone didn't beep nevertheless ring, however, Faye shamelessly lifted the receiver and searched for a dial tone; it was there. Faye's mind started to dwell on the people she studied in school. All the great artists, writers, scholars, and poets whose worth weren't recognized until after their deaths. How their tragic lives were triumphed with people worshipping them and their work. For reasons she didn't understand, the thoughts of these people and their unfortunate lives brought comfort to her; it even excited her. Then, her eyes trailed away from her cap and gown as she searched every corner of her apartment with her eyes. She didn't know what she was looking for until she saw it; her prescription sleeping pills.

The bottle sat on her bar top neatly placed behind a glass vase; it was as if the bottle shined with promise. To Faye, they became more than sleeping pills but magic sleeping pills that would mystically cure all her problems. She felt her body lift up from the futon. She didn't remember walking to the bar, she just remembered being there, standing over the pills. Faye held the bottle of pills in her hand; to her they were the key that unlocked the door to love; instantly, they became her idol. She popped the top. Then, as natural as one would swallow a pill in pursuit of a good night's rest; Faye shifted her jaws apart and emptied the entire bottle in her mouth. She went to sleep hoping that when she woke, she would be somewhere where she was loved and where she felt beautiful.

But that didn't happen. As she fell deeper into sleep, she had nightmares. She saw a little girl being chastised. Her grandmother and Rose were there. So, was the rest of her town. They had her tied to a large apple tree. The tree was full of apples and seemed to be producing them every five seconds. The town was throwing the apples at the little girl and chanting "ugly girl, ugly girl". She cried out for help but every time someone would seem to be coming to her aid, they picked up an apple and flung it at her face. Then Faye looked up and saw herself, staring and watching. The little girl cried out to Faye and Faye saw herself run up to her as if to guard her little body but when she reached close enough, she too picked up an apple and flung it at the little girl's face. Hitting the little girl felt both good and painful. But when the little girl cried out, the voice sounded so familiar it shook Faye. Faye looked closer and realized that the little girl tied to the tree was her. She jumped back; just as if she had seen a ghost. Then another apple appeared in her hand. Faye saw herself raise her elbow. The town continued to chant and push her to throw the apple. Just when she was about to fling it, she heard another familiar voice. This time she wasn't dreaming.

"Are you up?" Faye tried to focus on the figure that hovered over her body. She was so drowsy. Her head throbbed. IV needles hung out of her veins and plastic tubes where stuffed in her nostrils. Once she had her focus, she noticed that the voice was Rose. Rose held her make-up compact in one hand and a fashion magazine in the other. She carelessly dangled the objects over Faye's body. The scent of her perfume nauseated Faye. "Are you, okay?" Rose whispered. Faye didn't respond. "Is this about the graduation? I got so caught up that it literally slipped my mind and you know granny hasn't been feeling well lately," Rose spoke so quickly she stuttered, "That's why she couldn't make it today." Rose barely made eye contact with Faye while she gave her phony excuses. "Your doctor said that you should be fine. Your maintenance man found you. Can you believe that? Usually, they're never around when you need them." Rose laughed uneasily.

Rose's jokes didn't lighten the mood and she began to look as if she were cracking under pressure. Rose was never good at handling things on her own and she wasn't good at being the person who wasn't in need. She stepped away from the bed and took a seat in the guest chair. She nervously flipped through the pages of the magazine with an awkward smile on her face. "Your doctor's really nice," Rose pushed the magazine to the side. She began to admire her reflection with her make-up compact. She shined her teeth with her fingers and stroked her long hair. "He's cute too. I don't think he's married," she kept her eyes on the small round mirror. "Think I'll make a good doctor's wife?" She perked up her chest and flashed a quick flirtatious smile. "Granny surely would be thrilled. I don't know...I always saw myself marrying a lawyer. Don't know why. I guess I just like an aggressive man. Oh, and I look good in a business suit," she winked.

Faye listened to Rose babble on about herself while she flirted with her reflection in the mirror; she wished that Rose would leave. Seeing her intensified the very feelings that made her feel inadequate enough to end her life. It was then that she realized her plans didn't go through. Even the universe had rejected her. Faye felt her tears build up, but they never relieved her by flowing out, and then came the emotional tension and the instant burning of her eyes. She looked at Rose who was now filing her nails; she got angry. She wanted to lash out. Faye yanked out the tubes that were tapped to her nostrils; Rose screamed. Then she began to tug at her IV.

"You don't want to do that," A voice said from the door. Rose jumped to her feet and adjusted her mini skirt.

"Doctor…" She said in a girlish 'you saved the day" tone. If Rose hadn't addressed him, Faye would have mistaken him for an angel. His white coat looked so pure and bright it was almost blinding. He looked at Faye in a way that no person had ever looked at her. His mahogany colored pupils were tuned directly into hers without a distraction not even a blink. It was as if he was seeing inside of her. Faye looked away; she didn't want him to see inside her or outside her; she felt like Medusa, like she would turn him to stone. "Faye, this is the doctor. The one I was telling you about," Rose said with a flirty smile. He paid no attention to Rose. He walked right past her without even glancing in her direction. He kept his eyes fixed on Faye.

"You don't want to take these out too soon," he said while adjusting the tubes back under her nostrils. In the process, his knuckles brushed up against the bridge of her nose; he felt like silk. He put his hand on top of Faye's hand and stroked away the soreness from the IV. He had a healing touch that cured her from the inside out. Faye felt a small spark that ignited in her chest. When he stroked her forehead, it exploded throughout the rest of her body. Faye had crushes before, but this felt like more. Even if it never went past the day in the hospital, it reminded her that she was alive. It gave her something to hope for and Faye knew that people can survive a lifetime off just a grain of hope; even false hope.

A week later, Faye was back at her apartment. Everything was still in the perfect order she left it in. Her cap and gown hung neatly on the door and the empty bottle of pills sat neatly on the bar top. Faye sat in the same spot on her futon where she had her epiphany of death. Things in her life started to fall back in the same familiar order she was used to until three taps echoed from the opposite end of her front door. No one ever visited Faye and she wasn't expecting any packages. Faye opened the door and it was him; the doctor. He stood in her doorway holding a yellow carnation and a card; she felt like Cinderella and he was her prince. Faye faced him with her mouth open. Maybe he was there looking for Rose; it had to be a mistake.

"Hi," he handed her the flowers and peeked through the door into her apartment like he was searching for someone. Maybe Rose?

"Hi," Faye's voice cracked. "Who are you looking for?"

"You," he said softly. He stared at her the same way he had in the hospital. This made Faye nervous. Maybe she had died and this was her heaven. "I just wanted to check on you. Make sure you're okay," His tone was casual as if he had known her for years. He was forward; he let himself in the door. Faye didn't oppose. "By the way, my name is Randall."

"Ran...," she couldn't get the words out of her mouth.

"Randall," he helped her. "Shouldn't be too hard to remember."

Faye didn't understand how a man like Randall could ever be interested in her and for the first time in her life she didn't try to. She figured that this was God's overdue present to her. Her grandmother always said that God worked in mysterious ways. Maybe Randall was the mystery. All the years she spent praying for God to change her, to make her perfect so she could get a man wasn't necessary. Instead he sent her perfection, in the 6ft frame of a man named Randall. Faye's grandmother would definitely approve of Randall's fair skin and curly hair. Maybe Randall would finally give Faye's grandmother a reason to love her. Instantly, Faye started to fantasize about how their children would look. They definitely would have his hair and skin. Faye finally felt complete.

WHENEVER FAYE SHIFTED her body or showed any signs of life through subtle movements, Randall would plaster his size twelve boot on her abdomen, securing her from fleeing. He continued to take long drags of his cigarette, using her as his ashtray. The heat of the warm ashes landing on her skin, kept her alert. Her body jolted upward like someone had placed a defibrillator on her chest. "You know you're about worth as much as this cigarette," he chuckled, "and I only got half of it left." He lowered himself towards her and then shoved the lit cigarette in her face. "You want a smoke, you look like you can use a smoke." He chuckled again, this time louder. "Just when I thought you couldn't get any uglier, you go and prove me wrong. Ha!"

He flung the cigarette bud in her direction and began to clap his hands. The sound startled her and she jumped causing Randall to press down on her harder with his shoe. "Actually, this look works for you. See, I helped you again. You still think you're better than me?" He pressed his boot deeper into her abdomen. Faye bit down on her swollen lip to control the pain. "I saved your life. Me," he pounded on his chest. "No one would have cared if you died, you didn't exist before me. Your life was so dark and depressing, just like your skin." He let out an evil chuckle, "I brought you out. If it wasn't for me you wouldn't have that fancy ass bank job or this overpriced house. You wouldn't look down on me like a snob."

The things Randall said to Faye were harsh; the words were both the truth and a lie at the same time. Faye did accomplish those things after she started to date Randall. It was like Randall revived her after years of existing as the living dead. A month after they started dating, it was as if God pressed the fast forward button on her life. She was no longer stuck in a time warp. Being with Randall, just standing next to him in the store, validated Faye's existence on earth; it was the closest she would ever get to being beautiful herself and sometimes, during random moments, she actually felt beautiful. Although Randall never told her she was beautiful; the feeling became addictive. It followed her as she interviewed and received a top position at one of the largest chain of banks in the country. It lingered in the air as she spoke to people on the streets and interacted with co-workers and before she knew it, she had a life. Faye bought a house big enough for Randall to move in and a brand new Benz to confirm her success. Pretty soon, it looked as if Faye had it all. The man, the house, and a great career and people began to respect her for that without even taking notice to her outer appearance. People no longer looked at the part of Faye that she thought the world considered to be ugly but they looked at her wallet and respected that first. However, her money and status was a very thin veil she wore; almost see-through.

Her confidence began to develop the more she went to work. When she got a promotion after only six months on the job, her confidence level skyrocketed and it stayed at a consistent level, no more wavering. Randall noticed this change in her and didn't like it. He began to work against her. His cruel comments and the disrespectful way he treated her in public was how he began to bring her back down to the level where he could control her. She remembered the day that old familiar feeling of defeat and hopelessness began to fall back on her. It was during one of his poker games.

Faye loved when Randall had friends over. He never took her anywhere and declined every time she asked him on a real date, not just a trip to the grocery store. His poker night became her date night although she wasn't allowed in the room with him and the guys. She didn't care. It was the closest she was going to get to a public relationship with him. Faye got all dolled up with makeup and all. She spent hours in the kitchen making little sandwiches and even frying chicken wings for him and his friends. She wanted his friends to see what a good woman he had, but it wasn't his friends that had the problem recognizing her worth; it was him.

THE SOUND OF *the men laughing themselves energized Faye's mood. She couldn't help but feel somewhat responsible for the enjoyment that dwelled in the air. She bopped her head to the tune that buzzed in her earphones as she arranged tortilla chips neatly around a bowl of homemade cheese dip. She heard the men compliment Randall on how great the food was. "Yeah, it's alright," he acknowledged with mouth full of her sandwiches.*

"I can't even get my girl to boil water for a pot of tea. You got a good thing here."

"I'm gone have to agree with you on that," Faye smiled wide. "All I do to make it work for me is keep a garbage bag on my night stand."

"What?" The men chuckled and asked why. They were confused.

"They come in handy when it's time for me to do my deed. Nice cover up." The men roared with laughter. Faye's smile faded.

"I don't know, man. Me, I like a fine woman. Makes it better."

"Me and you are different. You drive a Lexus and I drive a Pinto. To the untrained eye your Lexus may seem better than my Pinto but it's not and let me tell you why," Randall's tone got serious as he philosophized, *"Your Lexus gone give you an expensive note to pay,"* he paused, *"shoot, maintenance is going to be a bitch. Because it's a Lexus and you paying all this money for it you gone feel obligated to take it out, drive it around, showing it off to the town. Then, everybody gone want a ride. Some may even try to steal it. That's a lot of work but my Pinto,"* he slapped a card on the table, *"My Pinto is paid for, low maintenance, no pressure to drive it around cause nobody want to see it any way. It's comfortable, it's reliable, and nobody gone want to ride it. I can just leave it in the garage, take it out, and oil it at my leisure,"* The guys laughed. Some of the men were laughing so hard they knelt over in their chairs and grabbed their stomachs. Faye knew that she was the Pinto that Randall was referring to. Faye knew that no matter how hard she tried, how much make up she caked on her face, Randall would never see her in the way she hoped. However, she had something he liked and it worked. After all, beggars can't be choosers.

"RANDALL," FAYE MURMURED. She could barely spread her lips to speak. They were almost swollen shut.

"What, Faye?" He yelled. Faye didn't know what to say to him. For the first time in their relationship, she was out of ways to calm him. No comments to stroke his ego, nothing to compliment him on; she was fresh out of defense tactics. This was a first in their relationship.

Dating Randall was like a game of emotional Russian roulette. She knew his moods even better than she knew her own, but they were hard to predict. When his face drooped, Faye knew that he was depressed and needed to have a long conversation that usually ended in a pep talk from her. Faye knew just the thing to say to get him to open up. Usually a simple, "Are you okay?" worked but sometimes Randall made her work for a response. She would start throwing out questions, ending them in compliments. "Is it work? It can't be work because you're so good at what you do." Or "Is it the test you're worried about because I know you can pass it. I know some really dumb doctors, they're nothing like you." She knew that after a round of questions, sooner or later his arrogant modest ways would open the door for hours of conversation. He would always open his response with "yeah but..." "Yeah but...they don't respect me at work." He was insecure in the worst way. Even more insecure than her.

This was when he was most vulnerable. Faye loved it because she felt that she was in control and it was the rare times that he showed affection to her; in his own selfish way. She would affectionately massage his shoulders and nod and smile and disagree with the negative things he was saying, however, she had to be careful with his vulnerable side because she knew that his vulnerability could quickly switch to violence just by using the wrong adjective. She remembered the first time he hit her.

 ～୨

Faye found Randall sitting in the dark. They were supposed to be going on their first date although they had been dating almost two months. Nothing fancy. A drive-in movie, complete with drive through food. But Faye was excited. Until she saw Randall soaking. He sat on her leather sofa in a pathetic slump. His hand supported the weight of his head. He stared off into space with his head tilted in the direction of the ceiling.

"Is everything okay, Randall?" She switched on the light. Randall squinted his eyes and used his hands to cover his face as if the lights were blinding him. "I'm sorry," she replied quickly as she switched the lights back off.

She stumbled in the dark, using her hands to guide her way to him.

"No," Randall groaned.

"You want to talk about it?" Faye walked cautiously in his direction. She slowly took a seat on the couch next to him.

"I can't see," Randall whined.

"Okay," Faye jumped up and flipped the switch again. Randall didn't squint this time.

"My throat is dry," he gestured towards his neck. Faye rushed to the kitchen and came back in seconds with a glass of cold water. Randall held up the glass and turned up his nose.

"Is this faucet water?" He asked cruelly.

"No…I know you can't stand the taste of water from the sink." Faye quickly responded. Randall shoved the glass back to Faye. Some of the water from the glass spilled out and landed on his bare toes. He grimaced as if the water were hot. Faye knelt down and cleared the water from his feet with her hand.

"Juice," he demanded before leaning back into the couch. When Faye returned, Randall had his face buried in his hands. He rocked back and forth and mumbled random words under his breath.

"Randall…I have your juice." He shooed Faye away with his hand. Faye put the glass on the coffee table. She sat down beside him. He eased his head down into her lap.

Faye felt needed. She liked this feeling.

"I have that test tomorrow."

"Your medical exam?" Faye asked softly. Later in their relationship, Faye learned that Randall wasn't quite a doctor yet. He was only an intern with the hospital. They allowed him to help out until he passed his exam. His father was one of the lead medical directors at the hospital. This put even more pressure on Randall.

"What other exam could I be talking about Faye?" he snapped. "If I don't pass this time…he'll definitely be through with me. He won't pay for a third attempt. I don't know what's wrong with me." He pounded on his forehead with his fist. "Why can't I ever do anything right?" He began to sob. Faye placed her hand on top of his forehead to block his punches. She softly massaged his temples in attempts to try and calm him.

"You shouldn't worry about the third time because you're going to get it this time. Statistics show that over half the people taking these tests fail on their first try," She whispered. Randall stopped sobbing. *"Look at all the great doctors of the world. They never mentioned their test scores or even their grades. A test can't define you, Randall. Only you can define you."* She continued to massage his temples. When she had seen how calm he was getting, she decided to take it a step further. *"Even your father can't even define you. Cause if he would see what I see, he would...."* Randall jumped up.

"Who mentioned anything about my father?" His brow lowered into the shape of a V and four thick wrinkles bulged from his forehead like oversized worms. His eyes widened with rage and Faye felt like she could feel the heat from his flaring nostrils blowing onto her. *"MY FATHER LOVES ME!"* The rage in his voice shook Faye. He rolled off the couch and headed towards the door. Faye followed behind him. Randall never mentioned his father, at least not directly.

During one of his random emotional breakdowns, he told Faye that he was the oldest of three children. His two younger siblings, both boys were working doctors already. They went through medical school quick and with ease. Randall had more trouble. He started two years ahead of them and finished a year after them. He couldn't handle the pressure and had to sit out a semester or two; this added up and held him back. He always felt like his father was ashamed of him, like he would never measure up to the man his father demanded him to be. Randall also told Faye that he was adopted. His mom and dad thought they couldn't have children. Then two years after, they had Rayman and the following year they had Richard. Randall grew up envying both his brothers and it wasn't long before that envy evolved into hate.

"I know he does, Randall. That's not what I meant," Faye defended herself; a tactic she would later learn to avoid. *"I just meant..."* Randall cut off her explanation with a powerful punch landing directly onto the soft part of her eye. The impact of his fist meeting her eye was so strong; it pushed Faye back onto the couch. She used her hand to block her fall but instead it shattered the glass of juice, cutting into her flesh.

The actual punch was quick in impact and sudden in timing. A simple *balling of his fist and the proper angling of his elbow, and she was out. But to Faye it was a long time coming. She was actually relieved he hit her. She had been expecting it during the course of their entire relationship. Faye learned all of Randall's boundaries and limitations. She had an idea of what situations may be too much for him to handle; tonight, he could finally learn hers. Faye had been waiting on it. It was her chance to show Randall how much she loved him and how unconditional her love for him was. It gave her a chance to prove to him that she would never leave him.*

Randall held out the cordless phone, "Call the police. It's what you want to do, right?" his tone was snide. "Here," he dangled the phone over her head, "take it." Faye snatched the phone and threw it onto the couch. She used the table to lift her weight off the floor. Randall grabbed her hand and examined her wound. "I have some gauze in the car. I'll get it," His tone was casual and he didn't rush as he casually walked out the front door like he was going to get the mail. He returned with his medical bag. "Okay, have a seat," he spoke to her as if she were his patient. "Let me take a look at that eye." His touch felt gentle again as he softly used her chin to turn her face towards him. "You were right, Faye," he dabbed around her bruised eye with cotton ball. "I shouldn't let a test define me. I'm good at what I do."

He never apologized and Faye didn't need him to.

FAYE DIDN'T NOTICE that she dozed off. When she came to, Randall was sitting across from her. His body cowered over with his legs welded deep in his chest and his face buried in between his knees. He rocked back and forth mumbling under his breath as he swallowed his silent tears. "Faye. You awake?" His voice cracked. Faye watched him without saying a word. She watched his lips tremble and his eyes lock into her eyes. They looked so empty, so dead. She watched him as he looked at her, waiting for her to revive him, for her to bring him back to life through her uplifting words. Faye broke away from his gaze. When her eyes turned, Randall began to sob heavily. "No one cares. No one cares, Faye. He won't even talk to me. They're not going to let me take the test again. It was the third time, Faye!" He yelled. "You don't care. I want to die, I want to die." It was at that moment that Faye realized she had everything twisted.

All the time Faye thought she was alone in studying him, she didn't realize that he was studying her, too. She always thought that she was the powerless one, the one that needed him to survive; the weak one but she was wrong. He needed her. The constant verbal abuse, the emotional strain he inflicted on her daily, the beatings she endured; it was all an act. Assaulting her then doctoring up her wounds; it was all perfectly executed to fit the illusion he created. The illusion that created the idea that she needed him. The illusion that evolved way past emotional control but tapped into her mental dependency; she was a victim of his trickery.

"Are you going to call the po…police, Faye?" He raised his head then dropped it back down like it was too heavy for him to hold. "Just do what you want," he waved his hand. He reached up towards the edge of the counter and reached for his bottle of liquor. When he saw that it was empty, he threw the bottle, it shattered across her tile floor. Faye didn't jump from the loud sound; she was surprised, however, she wasn't the only one. When Randall noticed she didn't get startled, the look in his eyes changed. He looked spooked. He grabbed onto the countertop and pulled himself off the floor.

Faye knew that he was trying to plan his next move. "I don't give a damn if you call the police," he yelled. "Maybe I'll make it easy for you. I'll just let them find you and you don't have to worry about calling them." He threatened her life. He forced himself to chuckle. He stomped his way to the refrigerator and slung open the door. "I outta make you get up and fix my drink," He bent over the refrigerator and rummaged through the shelves. "Where's my damn, beer?" Randall knocked items off the racks and broke every glass container he could find. Faye still didn't jump. She didn't stare at him but through him; through the charade that used to pump her full of fear. She knew that she was making him nervous. "You probably jinxed me. You didn't want me to pass that test because you knew I'll leave you. You think I'm going to be with you as a doctor? Ha! You were my punishment for not passing the test the first time. My motivation that reminded me how my life would be if I didn't pass the test." He continued to search through the shelves, creating even more of a mess.

His words didn't affect Faye. She was unmoved by his cruelness. Faye saw him clutching something in his hand before facing her. He raised his arm and aimed the object at her face. "You ugly bitch," he said. Faye knew exactly what he was clutching in his hand before he even threw it, an apple. She instantly remembered her dream. The dream where the little girl begged for her help.

Faye had an epiphany. It came to her just as quick as the first one she had when she wanted to die except this time she had the urge to live. She remembered that little girl, the little girl that everyone shunned, the little girl they chastised, the little girl they called ugly. The same little girl who despite all the ridicule, never let her heart go bitter, never held grudges and travailed in a world with no love. Faye began to cry, but not because she was afraid, or sad, or hurt from wounds he inflicted on her, both emotional and physical but because of her epiphany. The epiphany that took her 27 years to realize. A realization that was there all along but hidden under the skin they called ugly and lost in the world's perception of beauty. She realized she had something that wasn't temporary like the world's version of beauty but something immortal that she would pass down to her future generations, something that beauty could never mimic or replace; she had strength and that was the real beauty. Faye realized that strength had no look; it was faceless. It was a feeling. A feeling so powerful it grew in her bones and infected the blood in her veins. A power so strong that in the midst of chaos, she could find an inner peace.

Faye saw the apple flying towards her. She calculated in her head the amount of time she had before it reached her; she knew it was a matter of seconds. Physically, her body felt weak and heavy from the burden of pain but her spirit was stronger than ever. So strong that she raised the arm that she was sure he broke, spread her swollen fingers, and caught the apple. Randall gasped. He stood in front of her with his mouth open. His lips moved up and down but no words were formed. Faye gripped the apple tight in her hand. It was like it fueled her with strength. She lifted herself off the floor without stumbling. "What... you...think?" he stuttered. She could taste his fear and the flavor was sweet. "Who do you think you are? You're ugly. Your own family is ashamed of you," he spoke quickly as if his words were going to stop her in her tracks. "I'm going to finish you once and for all." He started his way towards Faye, she didn't step back nevertheless budge; it was too late, she called his bluff.

When he got close enough, he balled his fist, but Faye pulled open her utensils draw and grabbed a butcher knife. It stopped Randall right in his tracks. He lowered his raised arm but kept his fist balled. "Who are you calling ugly?" Faye whispered loudly. She held the pointy side of the knife towards Randall's neck. Randall held up his arms before falling to his knees. "Faye, don't. Please don't." Randall cried out. Faye pointed the blade closer to his neck. Randall's body shook as he sipped in air. "Please, Faye. Please." She stuck the point into his flesh just enough to prick him. "Help!" he screamed. Her hands craved his blood; she wanted to shove the knife deeper into his neck, so deep that she wouldn't be satisfied until he gagged and choked on his own blood. "Help," his cries got faint.

Looking down at his trembling body didn't excite her but disgusted her. He never looked so pathetic to Faye; it was as if she were seeing Randall for the first time. Her disgust quickly changed to sympathy, as she remembered her dream again. The little girl pleaded and no one came to her aid. She looked down and no longer saw Randall's 6ft frame but that of herself. Herself as the little girl begging for help; she saw herself in Randall but the lost version. The version of herself without strength or love to get her through. Faye felt for him. She lowered the knife. "Ugly only exists in the minds of the weak. And I'm not weak, Randall. Not anymore." She rubbed the top of his head. Randall wrapped his arms around her legs and sobbed. "Faye...help me."

"I can't help you anymore, Randall. You need to go and I don't ever want to see you again."

"Why...Why Faye? Please!"

"Because you're ugly, Randall," she said calmly. She looked down at him and pulled away. "Because you're too ugly for me." Faye kicked him off her. He fell back onto the floor and positioned himself in the fetal position. He sobbed like a baby. Faye dropped the apple to his side. "Take your apple and go." When he didn't move, she raised the butcher knife and stabbed the center of the apple. "GO!" she yelled. Randall jumped. He crawled his way out the door; sobbing all the way. When she heard the door slam behind her she pulled herself into the bathroom.

Faye stared at her reflection in the mirror. Through her swollen eyes, busted lips, and bruised emotions she thanked God. He had finally given her what she had been asking for since she was a small child; she woke up beautiful. The blessing just wasn't delivered in the package she expected, nevertheless she got it.

This blessing felt extra special because most people could not receive it. To others, beauty was only surface deep. But Faye was blessed with the ability to see beauty. Not the world's version of beauty but her true organic beauty.

The End

Love Licks

WATCHED THE LITTLE boy pull my seven-year-old daughter, Oliva, off the sliding board by her ankle. She was forced down the slide and came to a crashing end. The back of her head bounced hard against the grass. Olivia hopped up and giggled, rubbing the back of her head, trying to hold back tears while giving the little boy a dreamy-eyed gaze; she liked him.

Before Oliva allowed a tear to escape from her eye, the boy pushed her and she fell down, hitting her head against the slide. When she couldn't take anymore abuse, Oliva held the back of her head and ran to me for comfort. With tears in her eyes, she asked,

"Mommy, why Ben keep hitting if he likes me? Monica told me that her mom said that when a boy hits you that means he likes you. She said it's called love licks. Is that true?"

I looked down at my daughter. The innocence that shined behind her tear-glazed eyes struck a nerve. Monica's mom was feeding her lies. The same lies my mother fed to me. I pulled my daughter into my chest and embraced her. Hoping that she would feed off my strength. Then I lifted her chin so that she was looking me directly in the eye and I responded,

"There is no such thing as love licks."

My daughter looked at me and smiled like my words completed a puzzle in her mind. I watched her run back to the playground with a new understanding of truth. Then I had a flashback.

I REMEMBERED THE ten-year-old terror in my neighborhood; a boy named Bradley. He would pull on my pony tails, kick me in the knees, and pinch me wherever he could grab skin. There wasn't a day that went by that I didn't get assaulted by Bradley. All the other little girls had a crush on him. Whenever he came around, they would blush and try to get him to chase them. But it was me that he would push off the swings and yank from the monkey bars. I remember when I finally had enough of him. I was hanging upside down on the monkey bars, minding my own business like the rest of the kids at the playground. Then here comes Bradley eager to harass me. He kicked me in the back causing me to lose my grip on the metal bars. I fell and landed head first onto the grass, scraping my skin against a rock. The fall left a nasty scar across my forehead that I still have today. The once thick welt is a lot thinner and every year it becomes less visible but nevertheless it's still there; in more ways than one. When I look at it, I think of Bradley and what mamma told me.

My mamma said, "Veronica, don't worry bout that little nappy head boy. He just hitting you cause he like you. Those ain't nothing but love licks. It's just his little way of saying, he loves you. You got to get used to boys. All of them ain't gone express themselves the way we women do. Some gone show they feelings in other ways." I never forgot how I felt after that. Not only did I feel relieved but I felt special. Her words stuck to me like glue.

Out of all the little girls in the neighborhood, Bradley had chosen me to give his love licks to and I couldn't wait for the next one no matter how bad it hurt. From then own, when I saw Bradley coming, I slowed down a few paces, making it easier for him to catch up to me and whack me across the head or punch me in the back. The harder he hit, the more I felt he liked me. So I endured it. Understanding the burn from the pain of his fist was ignited by the flame from his love. After a while, the pain started to feel like love so much to the point where I couldn't distinguish between the two.

It was then that I decided that love was supposed to hurt. I remember when my daddy would give my mother love licks. It never was anything too harsh and wasn't too often but it happened from time to time. A yank, a push or sometimes a slap across the face but the slaps were always rare. When he hit her, it never failed that the next day he would come home with roses and chocolates and teddy bears; it was like Valentine's Day. He would give her hugs and kisses and whisper things in her ear and it would be like they were on their honeymoon again; opposed to the usual behavior of my father coming home from work, barely grunting two words to her and retiring in front of the TV. Mamma seemed happier after the licks, too. She would finally comb her hair and put on a nice dress to wear around the house. It was like those licks were the spice to heat up their relationship when it had gotten too dull. Even at a young age, I grew to anticipate the next time daddy hit mamma. One day of pain brought in at least three days of joy; I looked forward to it just like I'd looked forward to Bradley hitting me. Somehow, it tied into my happiness.

So, it was no surprise that after dating several straight forward and what society would label as respectable gentlemen, I got bored. Without love licks, there was no spice. I wasn't sure if they were really into me. I tried to push their buttons in every possible way and neither of them as much as breathed hard on me. I thought that it was something wrong with me. That they didn't love me enough and I was actually hurt by the fact that they didn't give me any love licks. Then I met, Jacob.

In the beginning, I almost marked Jacob off my list. He was what I call the movie perfect gentleman. So much to the point where he didn't seem real. He opened doors. We had candlelight dinners. He bought me fresh flowers and we took long walks in the park. He wooed me in a way that the average woman only experienced through TV or a romance novel, yet I wasn't satisfied; little did he know, it didn't take all that for me. A box of chocolates and flowers weren't enough for me. I needed something real. Something I could feel.

It was right at three months into our dating that I decided to push his buttons as far as I could. I started to test the waters to see what it was that made him tick. I learned from the way he behaved while we were out that he didn't like men looking or talking to me too much. He would make little comments like, "Man, he was really checking you out," or, "Dang, he had to do a double take when you got up". I thought it was cute because he didn't seem too mad but somehow I knew his half jokes were a cover for how much he hated it.

One day when we were out, I actually smiled back at a man who he considered to be flirting with me. Jacob looked at me and smiled and that was it. Strike one against him. Strike two came when we were out at a club and I actually drifted off and purposely lost myself on the dance floor, leaving him at the table to watch me bumping and grinding with other men. Still no reaction. "Did you have fun?" He asked calmly. After that, I was going to give him one more chance but little did I know strike three would never come.

It happened when I wasn't even trying to entice him; it really caught me off guard. I should have seen it coming though. After the last two incidents, Jacob had become withdrawn from me. He wasn't as attentive and he became more distant with each visit. I didn't care though because I was about to mark him off my list anyway.

I was sitting on his couch watching a movie with him when my cell phone rang halfway into the movie. I pulled the phone out of my purse and saw that it was my mother so I ignored the call, stuffing the phone back in my purse. I didn't know it then but Jacob was watching me. The phone rang a second time as it usually did when my mother couldn't get me the first time. This time when I reached in my purse to grab my phone, Jacob jumped up, snatched the phone out of my hand and threw it against his wall, cracking the screen. Without hesitating, he yanked me up by the collar and slapped me so hard I fell back onto his couch. I'll never forget the look in his eyes; he looked deranged. I had never seen a man flip so quickly. I instantly took his anger for passion and thought to myself, he must really be into me.

Then his look changed. He looked at me quizzically as if he was studying my reaction. Waiting to see what I was going to do so he would know what to do. I gave him what he wanted and what I thought I needed, I said, "I'm sorry. It was just my mother, Jacob. I'm sorry." It was the perfect reaction; it was the perfect invitation for him to hit me again. I couldn't have planned it better myself. That was the day we committed ourselves to each other. We were married within the next two months.

The first year of our marriage was just an extension of the relationship we had before. We didn't waste any time defining one another; we just stepped into our self-assigned roles. He was the dictator and I was his humble follower. Whatever he said went and I liked it. I thought it was cute that he cared about me so much that he monitored my calls, picked out my clothes, and made me ask for permission before I went out. I thought he did this because he didn't want to lose me. Because he saw something in me that I didn't see in myself and he treasured it so much that he had to protect it the best way he could.

At first, his controlling ways were subtle. The day he decided to choose my wardrobe he did it in a clever yet romantic way. He would always tell me that I was so attractive that men couldn't help themselves so I had to help them the best way I could by not wearing form fitting jeans or low cut shirts. He said that he wouldn't allow a strange man to lust after his wife. To make it less controlling he said that he knew it wasn't my fault that God made me so attractive and that he just felt so honored and blessed to be the one that has me. He said that the other men didn't deserve that honor because I was given to him and him only. I knew that it was extreme but he said it in such a cute way that he made me feel like a precious jewel.

One day, I came home from work and my closet was empty. All my shoes, clothes, purses; everything was gone. He told me, "I wanted to surprise you with a little shopping spree. I went ahead and bought you all new things because you deserve the best. I was getting tired of seeing you in those old clothes." He seemed so excited about the surprise that I ignored the fact that everything he picked out couldn't be farther from a reflection of my taste. It looked like he had gone to the Misses section in Wal-Mart and picked out everything they sold that was baggy, long, and knitted. I thanked him with a kiss and bright smile.

It was just the idea that he would make the attempt to buy me a new wardrobe that flattered me regardless of his dated style. Besides, I didn't want to discourage him from taking the initiative to surprise me in the future. My mamma would always say, 'girl, you better take what you can get from a man when they offering and when you get it act like it is gold even if it is brass cause brass is better than dirt.' So, I wore the clothes.

His next move was to get me to quit my job. I was the manager of a law firm. It was hard enough working a 9 to 5 with some weekends and overtime but when they switched my schedule to nights, Jacob wasn't having it. I didn't mind the night shift because it was slower than the day. Less work and it gave me time to myself but Jacob still made a big deal out of it and I let him. When I would come home he would look at me so concerned and sad as if I had been slaving in a cotton field all day. The second I walked through the door he would immediately take my bags as if I didn't have the strength to carry them. He would rub my feet and go on and on about how wrong the company was for working me so hard and how he just couldn't take it anymore.

Jacob knew I liked my job. He heard me tell the story several times about how I started as a receptionist and climbed my way up the corporate ladder to manager all within three years. It was what I was most proud of and what I was good at. I knew that I didn't have to work; that I had options because of Jacob's job. He was a physical therapist for athletes and he made plenty of money. I just worked because it was what I wanted to do. I knew that my days of working were over the night he woke me up at two in the morning. He was near tears. He told me, "I had a dream that you were working late at the firm and you were on your way home and you got attacked in the parking lot. You were screaming for me and I couldn't get to you," he sobbed although no tears fell. "I just couldn't get to you," he repeated and sniffed hard. "I can't take this anymore, Veronica. I just can't take this worrying. It's interfering with my work, with our marriage. You have to quit." I was so busy comforting him that somewhere in between my embracing him and his constant dry sobs, I said okay. So, that was that; I quit without giving a two weeks' notice.

The last thing he took from me was more valuable than my job: my friends. After I quit my job, we got a bigger house and he bought me a brand new car that we really couldn't afford after the loss of a second income but nevertheless, I was so excited that I didn't have time to miss my job or worry. When my friends would come over, he would always have negative things to say about them. Especially my best friend of 10 years, Nikki. He always said that Nikki was jealous of me and wondered why I brought her around.

He took it a step further when he pulled me to the side after our first house warming and told me that she made a pass at him. He said, "Veronica, I'm only telling you this because I hope you would tell me if you were in the same situation." Then he shook his head and said never mind and started to walk away before finishing his sentence. He practically made me beg him to tell me. After the third please, he blurted out, "Nikki made a pass at me."

Deep inside I knew that he was lying but I made myself believe that there was some form of truth there; maybe he was exaggerating or confused.

"I saw her at the hospital the other day," he said.

Nikki was a traveling nurse and sometimes they would end up in the same hospital.

"She asked me to go to lunch and I thought that there wouldn't be any harm in it because she is practically family. At lunch she went on and on about how blessed you are to have me and how she hopes that you don't mess things up with me and that you are treating me like you appreciate me. Then she grabbed my hand and told me that if I ever feel unappreciated she can help me out. Then she winked at me." When he said she winked, I knew that it was lie. The grabbing of the hand was a stretch but a wink wasn't even Nikki's style and neither was Jacob. Nikki hated him and thought he was too controlling but I had a choice to make. Mamma always said do what you got to do to keep your marriage, so I chose Jacob. To please Jacob I called Nikki in front of him and made a big scene and he loved it; I hated every bit of it and when I got a moment alone, I cried. I later wrote it off as one of the many sacrifices of marriage.

After he got rid of my job, ran my friends away, and had me on 24-hour surveillance, the love licks started to come more frequently and were more brutal. Before, it was as if we had almost planned them. It was our way of wining and dining; it was our foreplay. I would give him invitations to hit me by doing things I knew would trigger a physical response out of him. Usually, it was small things like complaining about his late nights at work. The complaining usually got him to jack me up against the wall or give me a slight shove. Disagreeing with him in public usually got me a slap in the car accompanied with an intimidating yell. "Look woman, you don't speak to me that way in front of people." He would bark at me. I would cower down in the passenger seat like a little scared puppy. It was acting; I felt like it was what we both needed. Afterwards, he would hug me and say that he was sorry.

Then next morning when I awoke, there would be a love note on my pillow. Usually a poem of him confessing his love for me and explaining to me why he gets so mad he has to hit me. He would basically say that he loved me so much that I made him crazy and I was the first woman he had ever laid hands on. I was the only one in the world that could trigger such anger in him. And of course, I felt special.

Then one day, he started hitting me without me complaining or our public disagreements. For some reason, these hits caught me off guard. Then the poems stopped coming and apologies went away; it didn't seem so romantic anymore. Especially when my love licks started to show. He started hitting me so hard and so often that his love showed all over my face. It showed around my eyes like sunglasses, big and dark circles. It showed around my neck like a necklace, red and blue welts, and it dripped out my nose like red roses. Most days, when I'd completed all his assigned chores and ran his errands, I didn't have anything to do but sit around the house all day and wait for him to come home. So, naturally I started to eat. I became a binge eating, soap opera watching couch potato.

This was a major change for me because I took pride in my looks before Jacob. I jogged, lived in the hair salon, and kept a five-pound limit on my weight gain. To my surprise I gained 20 pounds. It was like I looked up one day and was too big to wear my own underwear. Between the extra weight around my waist, the bruises on my face, and a broken spirit, I could barely recognize myself in the mirror. I started to feel pathetic and worthless, and it was like he sensed these feelings I was having because he started to tell me how pathetic and worthless I was; my damaged state gave him reason to hit me and made it easier for him.

His hits no longer felt like love but sorrow. He started pushing his own buttons and finding his own reasons to hit me. I no longer had to egg him on. Then I tried to figure out how to egg him off. I was doing everything I could to prevent him from hitting me but he always found a reason. Too much salt in the steak or I didn't iron all the wrinkles out of his shirts; any reason he could find. Other times he came home with liquor on his breath and with times like that he needed no reason; he became a brute.

He started to use the decisions he made for me, against me. "You so selfish that don't nobody want to be around you. Not your family or any of your friends. If you were such a loving person, then why don't they want anything to do with you?" I never answered his rhetorical questions; I knew they were just a set up. "You could at least try to keep yourself up. You gained all that weight and you dress like my grandma. I work too hard to come home to a granny wife. Especially when I can have any woman I want. You see, that's the problem," he would say, "you don't appreciate me. I got you this big ass house that you can't clean. Got you that fancy car and you just waste gas."

In his eyes, everything was my fault. When the incoming bills surpassed the incoming cash, he blamed me. He would say, "You so damn lazy. You just sit around the couch all day and watch TV. How easy it must be to be you. Making me feel sorry for you so that you could quit your job and mooch off me. You with your little manipulative plans. Now I got all this pressure on me."

The day he said that to me, I couldn't keep silent. My job was my life; it was what I was most proud of. I said back to him, "You made your bed and now it's too sloppy for you to lie in it. I don't have a lazy bone in my body. Hell, the energy it takes for me to take care of your emotionally unstable ass is enough work for me to call it my own business. I need to start filing a 1099 for this relationship and pray I get a refund check." Yelling that to him was the most I had felt like my old self since we had gotten married. He was shocked, offended and, best of all, hurt. When his eyes widened, mine closed because I knew what was coming, I didn't have to see. He whaled on me good that night but I didn't care. I felt relieved that he was hitting me for a reason and for a reason that I chose; just like it used to be except I was happy he was the one hurting for a change.

One day I decided to leave him. It wasn't thought out or premeditated, I just, all of sudden, had a rush of energy to pack my bags and leave. And I did. I didn't go far. Just 20 miles down the road to my parent's house. I never forget the way my mamma looked at me when she seen me standing at the door with my bags. It had been months since I've seen her or talked with her for more than two minutes on the phone. Her mouth didn't reveal what her eyes showed. "What you doing here?" She asked casually as if she had just spoken to me a couple of hours ago. She ignored my puffy black eye like it wasn't even there. She tried her best not to look at it. I didn't wear sunglasses on purpose. I wanted her to see what Jacob had done to me and I desperately wanted to see her reactions so I would know how to react. "What you got them bags for?" She asked. "And where Jacob?" She looked over my shoulder.

When I told my parents that I was going to marry Jacob, there was no scrutiny by my father or words of wisdom by my mother. It was just a simple, 'well that's nice' from my mother and shrug and a grunt from my father. They didn't ask why I loved him or how he made me feel. My father didn't integrate him or make him fear the consequences of hurting me. They just showed up to my wedding and smiled in the photos and ate the free food. My dad walked me down the aisle and handed me over to a stranger. Parents feel that their children need more protection when they're younger. They do all these things to ensure their safety. Coming in the house when the street lights come on. Not being able to go further than five blocks from your house. All the little things. But what about when your kids grow up? Who's there to call them inside when it gets too dark or to warn them when they're in a danger zone? I still need that protection.

"Marriage isn't a revolving door like your other relationships, Veronica," my mother said to me. "You can't just walk out when things get tough. It requires lots of strength and patience. Jacob may not be perfect but he a good man. Got a good solid job and he bought you that brand new house and car. He even help me and your daddy out from time to time. That's a good man. If you run away at the first sight of trouble, then you a weak woman. How do you know you ever gone get another man to love you like that? You gone be living a life of regret. Go back to your husband and work it out."

That was my mother's advice to me. She never mentioned my eye, but my father did. As soon he saw me he said, "Wow, that's a pretty big shiner you got there. What you do? Man aint gone raise his hand to you like that for nothing. You still spoiled Veronica. Everything can't be about you. Your husband working hard at the hospital providing for you, you got to learn to appreciate him more and keep yourself up. His price for being faithful shouldn't be coming home to a fat, lazy, complaining wife." So there I had it. Between my mother and my father I gathered that I needed to be stronger, endure more and appreciate him for all he does; even his punches. So, I returned home without him ever knowing that I left.

Later that night, I tried the best I could to spice myself up. I made a nice dinner, lit candles, and burnt incense. I took the advice from my parents to heart. When my father saw my eye and asked me what I had done, it was like I had an epiphany. What had I done? I started to reflect back and try to pinpoint when things started to change. My mother used to always say, 'instead of pointing the finger at someone else turn back on yourself and see what you get.'

Well, I did that and I made myself take more blame than I was giving him. I could have been cleverer when he was buying the new house and cars. Maybe sweet talking him into something more affordable so that he wouldn't be so stressed all the time. I should've kept myself up instead of just giving up and turning to the couch and refrigerator for companionship; I should have turned to him. I felt lucky that it wasn't too late for me. I could change things. So, I made the romantic dinner. When he came home that night, he actually looked surprised. He walked through the door and I immediately grabbed his bags. I took his coat and led him to the table; I treated him like a king and he soaked up every second of it. I massaged his shoulders as he ate. I did it because I thought it was thoughtful but he started to take the royal treatment to a whole other level. He dictated where and how hard I massaged his shoulders.

"More to the left, down, up, use your elbow not your hand." He finally slapped my hands away when he grew tired of me missing all the right spots. "Warm this back up," he said while handing me his plate. "And you put too much salt on this meat. You got any fresh meat left?"

I nodded.

"Go ahead, burn me up another steak." His tone wasn't harsh. He spoke so matter of fact although the things he said were harsh. He didn't appreciate the dinner. He treated it as if it were about time I had done this. Like he expected it. I just thought to myself, I'm gone have to try harder. Love aint easy. I told myself that this could be like a challenge. Before I met Jacob, I would set goals for myself. Where I wanted to be in my career, weight, mental, all kinds. It became a hobby that I was good at because I would set them and then achieve them. Achieving them felt so good; it made me feel complete as an individual, so powerful. It was going to feel good having that feeling again; I looked forward to it.

I started off small. Doing little things to get us back the way we were. I met my weight loss goal plus an extra five pounds. Of course, Jacob complained. He would say "who you trying to lose all that weight for?"

I would just smile and flirt the best I could. "You, baby," I would say while rubbing his head. During the hours I knew he was coming home, I made myself seem to be more active. I was always doing something. Every week I started and completed a project, anything to keep me busy. I tried my best to impress so that he seen that I wasn't lazy. Painting the house, cutting the lawn, I even refinished the wood floors. So when he stepped in the door, he could see me doing things and still have his dinner; that way he could see that I appreciated hard work. I tried so hard but things didn't get much better. Even through all that he found a reason to smack me. He got suspicious of me. "*Why you trying so hard? What's going on, Veronica? You messing around? Huh?*" He would interrogate me. He got so suspicious of me that I had to start checking in with him everywhere I went. When I went to the store and when I left the store. I felt like I was in the military. To feel better about the situation, I told myself that "at least he is interested in me again. When I had all that weight on me it was like he didn't care where I went. At least he's starting to recognize me again. He may have been controlling but he was recognizing my worth and in his own way was showing it to me."

I knew that my friends and other women would call me crazy, but I valued my relationship with Jacob. My motto was by any means necessary. I made my bed and I had to lay in it regardless of how dirty the sheets were. I did often wonder what made me make my bed the way I did. Why would I make my bed so uncomfortable that later I wouldn't want to lie in? It was the first time that I started to ask myself these questions. The more questions I asked the more I realized I had no answers. I started to become distant. It didn't last long though. I always wondered what would have happened if I kept interrogating myself with these questions. But the questions went away when I was late.

I felt more tired than usual and I was a lot more emotional. I wrote these feelings off by thinking to myself that I was overworking around the house. But then my period didn't come. I took two home pregnancy tests and confirmed it with a doctor before I started to have feelings about it. When the doctor confirmed that I was pregnant, I instantly felt a connection with my child. I felt like the child I held in my womb was the key that would unlock the missing happiness of my marriage. To my surprise, Jacob felt the same way. He embraced my belly and held me and his unborn child like we were precious jewels; it felt nice to feel that way again. To feel that way without first being hit felt more genuine. It was a feeling that I could get used to.

The first month Jacob instantly fell into father mode. He didn't want me on my feet too long. He actually encouraged me to stay home and watch TV; practically had me on bed rest. He started reading all these books on parenting and health for pregnant women. It was amazing. He was like a different man and I felt like a different woman. He didn't raise his hand to me, not even as much to swat a fly out my direction. I finally felt like a queen in my castle. I never knew he could be so gentle and soft spoken. For the first time in my life I finally felt like I had really done something right by getting pregnant. This whole experience had been a learning curve for me. Boy, had I been missing out all these years. I never knew that a soft word could feel so much sweeter than a hard hit. That him rubbing my stomach and stroking my hair so gently could make me feel more loved than him yanking me around and controlling my every move. I thought he desired me more when he would smack me around but the way I felt now, the sweet-gentle-kindness, didn't compare. Then one day a man with the wrong number called my cell phone.

I was two and a half months then. I was lying on my back while Jacob stroked my stomach and read to our child. He read our child books saying it would make the child smarter if the parents read to them and let them listen to classical music while they were in the belly. As he read, I was beginning to fall asleep when my phone rang. I looked at the screen and didn't recognize the number. Usually, I didn't answer numbers I didn't know but Jacob didn't like when I didn't answer the phone while he was around; it made him suspicious. So I answered.

The man on the other end of the phone had the deepest manly voice I had ever heard. It was so deep it trailed out the phone where Jacob could hear it. "How you doing, lady? I've been trying to call you all day." The man spoke to me like he knew me.

Jacob's mood instantly changed.

Shit, I thought to myself.

Jacob lifted up from the bed and leaned in closer to my phone. He studied my face quizzically as if he were searching for some hidden reaction or a clue that would suggest I knew the man. I had to be cooler than I had ever been in my life, even though I was nervous. "Sir,

I'm pretty sure you have the wrong number." I said with a clear voice. My heart was pounding so hard that I knew I was seconds away from stuttering my speech which would be the clue Jacob needed to strike me.

"Oh, this aint Trisha? I'm sorry I must have dialed the wrong number."

I hung up and lay back down as if nothing happened; Jacob didn't. He leaned up and stared down at me as if I were still talking to the guy. "What the fuck was that?" he said, accusing me.

"What?" I had to play it off, although I knew I was telling the truth.

"You don't want to play with me, woman; you know you don't." He shifted his feet to a fighting stance.

"*The phone call?*" I acted shocked. "It was a wrong number. You want me to call him back?"

Jacob continued to stare down at me. His brow was lowered into an evil v shape and his jaw was clenched tight. He looked down at my face as if I had the truth written under my skin. "It was just the wrong number, Jacob. That's all." Jacob didn't hit me then. He walked away angry; I was relieved.

A couple of days later, Jacob started to transition back into his old self. The special treatment stopped. No more rubbing on my belly or massaging my feet. He started to avoid me and when I was around him, he acted like everything I did annoyed him. He started to complain about me sleeping so much. He said I was teaching the child to be lazy. Then he started to complain about my cooking. My morning sickness lasted all day. Certain smells would trigger me the wrong way and I would gag and sometimes even throw up. Jacob hated when I did that. I explained to him that I couldn't control it but he would just say, "You not about to tell me you can't control that. How much damn attention do you need? You better try and control the shit around me."

So, I tried. It was hard but I tried. Until the day he requested I make him lamb chops for dinner. First, it was the look that my stomach didn't agree with. The pink red blood speckled flesh turned my stomach. Then it was the smell. It never bothered me before but being pregnant heightened all my senses and the lamb didn't smell like lamb anymore but dead animal; road kill. It started with a gag. I held it back. Then a cough. Then it was like an explosion. I threw up all over the kitchen floor before I could make it to the bathroom. Jacob charged into the kitchen yelling over my shoulder like a drill sergeant.

"Damn, girl. Didn't I tell you about this? You so nasty. What type of woman throws up all over the kitchen floor? Huh?" He grabbed the back of my neck and lowered my face into the vomit like he was training a dog. "This shit belongs in the bathroom." He shoved harder on my neck until my nose was in the mess. "In the bathroom," he repeated with a deeper shove. He let me go and grabbed a mop. He threw it at me. The metal handle bounced off my back. "Clean this shit and then go wash up. I lost my appetite."

I did as he said. I scrubbed the floor with Clorox to try and cover the odor. However, smelling the chemicals turned my stomach again. I almost choked on my own vomit trying to keep it down. It burned my throat to push it back down but the more I swallowed the more it would come up. Jacob must have heard me gagging because he came running back into the kitchen, waving his fist in the air. I held out my hands. One to protect my face and the other my stomach. "Jacob," I pleaded. "The baby. The baby."

He stopped himself and stepped back. "Probably aint my damn baby anyway." He whispered loudly before storming out the front door. I wasn't shocked to hear him make the allegation but I was surprised that he didn't hit me although I knew it was only a matter of time before he did. He'd found his reason again. I went to the bathroom to clean up before he returned. I stared at myself in the mirror. I started to feel pathetic again. Maybe I was foolish to think that the violence would be over so quickly. Then my eyes went to the old scar I had across my forehead. The one a 10-year-old Bradley had given me; my first love lick. I started to think and then I remembered how I felt before I knew it was a love lick, before I made it okay. I remembered how my forehead throbbed and burned with pain. How angry I was with

Bradley, and how much I hated it when he hit me, and how worthless and pathetic it made me feel. Kind of like how I felt now.

Then the questions started again. Except this time it was like they were coming from within. Like my unborn child was interrogating me. Why was it ever okay even after Mamma told me it was a love lick? Why did I suddenly feel special? Why the hits stopped hurting so bad and why I needed Jacob to hit me to validate our love? Then I started to wonder, at what point did the hits start to hurt again? Feeling my head throb and my cheeks burn with pain from the slaps no longer felt like love but hate. Why didn't I like it anymore? When did I start to become that annoyed little girl again?

Later that night, Jacob came stumbling in the house smelling like brandy and cigarettes. Now that he had his reasons again, I knew there was nothing I could do to avoid the fight. I felt him standing over me, I didn't move. I pretended to be asleep but I should have known better because that never worked in the past. He kicked the bed, but I still didn't move. Then he kicked harder; I didn't budge. So, he grabbed my arm and yanked me from under the sheets throwing me to the floor. "You be honest with me. Is that my baby you carrying?"

I knew Jacob knew it was his baby. He was just ready to play a game I quit playing a long time ago. I ignored him. I stood up and got back in bed. I pulled the sheets over my body real tight; I used them as a shield.

He struggled with them until he pulled me while wrapped in the sheets off the bed a second time. "Answer me." He demanded. He pulled me up from the floor and slammed me into the wall. "Answer me."

The smell of his breath started to make me gag but I didn't hold it back this time. I gagged and gagged until he pushed me out the door. I landed on the floor near the bathroom. I crawled in the bathroom and hovered over the toilet. "*You better get all that out.*" He stood over me yelling and cursing. He called me a whore and a slut. He called our child a bastard. The more he yelled, the more I began to feel like that little annoyed girl again. He pulled me up from the toilet and buried my face into the basin of the sink. He turned on the water and started to splash cold water on my face and mouth. He called me disgusting and lazy and a slob. "I never seen nobody gag and get on like you ever." Then I couldn't take it anymore. I gave him what he wanted. I gave him his reason; his reason on my terms. "I gag so much and throw up so much because the child in my stomach hates you. It hates to be around you. It hates when you touch me, it hates the smell of you. It hates you because it's not you. It's not you at all."

He grabbed my throat first. He squeezed the breath out of me. He clutched my neck while murmuring something under his breath. Maybe he was calling me a bitch or maybe a whore. I didn't care. He led me by my throat towards the stairs, then he let go. "It aint my baby?" He asked in a loud whisper.

I didn't respond. I saw him when he balled his hand up into a tight fist. I even saw when he raised his elbow but for some reason I couldn't move. It was just like the first time he hit me but I accepted his blow for different reasons. I didn't embrace it as a love lick but, for some reason, as freedom. I saw his knuckles in the air, lowering themselves toward my face. At least I thought it was my face. It wasn't my face, but my stomach. He punched me in the stomach so forcefully I fell backwards down the stairs and landed hard in the corner of the wall. I felt dizzy and my stomach cramped. It was our child's first love lick.

I had a choice to make: Jacob or my child. I knew there was nothing else I could do. I gave him the permission he needed to shit all over me. I knew Jacob wasn't going to change; he didn't have to. I allowed, encouraged, and motivated the hits in the beginning; it was a childish game I played with him and myself but it had to stop. Jacob didn't have to change, I did. On account of my unborn baby, I had to put away all childlike things and be a protector for her. My stomach continued to cramp and it was as if my child was yelling for me to protect her. Even in the womb, my child was already stronger and wiser than me. I watched Jacob slowly walking down the stairs. Then the questions started again. They came with every rumble in my stomach. It was as if my child were yelling them to me. I still didn't have the answers to the questions but I had the solution. I made my choice. My child wasn't the key to unlock our unhappy marriage but a key to free me from brutality. I used that key and I freed myself; I chose my child.

When Jacob got to the bottom of the steps, I had an epiphany. There was no such thing as love licks; there never was. My mother lied to me to excuse Father. To make his brutality alright. To normalize the ideology that love comes with pain. I pulled myself up from the floor. I didn't smile. I didn't frown. I just stared back at Jacob blankly.

Then I yelled, "There is no such thing as love licks!" I yelled it even louder the second time like I was trying to first convince myself. "There is no such thing as love licks!" I yelled and yelled and yelled until Jacob thought I was going crazy. "There is no such thing as love licks!"

Jacob finally got spooked enough and ran out the door. About an hour later I grabbed my things and ran out the door myself; I never returned.

I made a decision to teach my daughter all the things I learned the hard way. I wanted to be an example to her because I knew she was watching me like I was watching my mamma. I didn't allow her to believe in fairy tales; especially the ones that suggest a woman need protecting and saving by a man and, more importantly, I didn't allow her to believe in love licks.

The End

54

At Fault

"**Y**OU...YOU...," HER VOICE shook. Kina tried to form a sentence but the anger that blazed inside of her burned all her words like fire and her reasoning dissipated like ashes in the wind. She pointed her trembling finger at Angelo who stared past her with a wide eyed gaze. Mouth agape, Angelo felt as if someone had just knocked the wind out of him. Forgetting to breath, he searched for air. He couldn't respond to Kina. Fear struck his entire body with lightning speed. Shock radiated deep in his bones. This couldn't be happening to them.

Kina felt like someone had twisted the bottom out from her soul and all her insides plunged down into her stomach and boiled. She hovered over and sobbed heavy. Her red eyes strained. "Yo..yooou…" she stuttered. "YOU KILLED ME," she finally blurted out. Her screams shook the room. She squeezed the paper she held in her right until it crumbled to the size of a cotton ball. But that didn't change what was written on it. It didn't change their fate. "I gave up everything to be with you, Angelo. My entire life revolved around your needs. You were all I wanted. I…I…just wanted you!"

Kina strained her eyes to see Angelo through her tears. Angelo still couldn't make eye contact with her; it was as if she weren't in the room. Kina's crying and screaming bounced off him and faded in the background like white noise. Angelo felt alone. He slouched on the sofa chair with his shoulders hunched over his knees and his face lowered to the carpet. His honey brown complexion went pale. He disconnected himself from the world. Kina continued to yell.

"I lost 15 pounds for you…15 pounds in one month because you told me I was losing myself," she held out her index finger. "I put down five grand on your car and I made the payments for you for the first two months. I drove your mother back and forth from the doctor and took in your badass little sister until she destroyed everything I had. And I forgave you over and over and over again!" Her voice strained.

She sucked in a quick gulp of air and continued, "I tolerated your three-year-old child and his hateful mother. THREE YEARS OLD." She shoved three fingers in his face before planting them on his forehead and pushing his head back. "We been together five years and you have a three-year-old. I forgave you then and the time after that and the time after that. I JUST WANTED US TO WORK!" she screamed again. She fell to her knees like her emotions were too heavy to carry. "WHY? WHY DID I NEED YOU SO MUCH? WHY DID I LOVE YOU MORE THAN I LOVE MYSELF? WHY DID I SACRIFICE MY LIFE FOR YOU?" She pulled on her hair and pounded on the carpet. Kina was breaking down. "How could I allow you to do this to me?" her tone lowered. "I don't want to die!" she screamed again. "Not like this," she picked up the balled up paper and threw it at him.

"You couldn't just kill yourself? You had to bring me along for the ride? Why Angelo? Why?"

Kina pounded against the carpet but Angelo still didn't respond. He slowly shook his head like he was trying to wake himself from a nightmare. Angelo was in disbelief.

Kina buried her face into her knees and sobbed. She sobbed so hard, her body quivered and shook like she was having a seizure. The sight of Kina rolling around the carpet like she was trying to put out an emotional fire snapped Angelo back into reality. He tried to calm her down by placing his body on top of hers and embracing her. He squeezed her, letting her know that he was there but she kicked her legs and waved her fist in his direction, attacking him.

A forceful kick pushed him back towards the couch. His lower back hit against the bottom cushion. He felt himself disconnecting again. Kina kicked him and scratched him until his skin was under her nails. Angelo didn't flinch. He didn't protect himself. He didn't fight back. He couldn't feel the pain. At least not on the outside. Getting hit by a Mack truck would have felt better than this. This pain was unbearable; it was a special kind of fear. A feeling made from two ingredients: fear and shame. Angelo saw Kina's mouth moving but couldn't hear anything. He saw the spit from her mouth land on his face but he didn't wipe it. He saw her claws stretching out towards his face but he didn't dodge her. Angelo was paralyzed. Everything was happening in slow motion. Everything except what brought them to this moment. The flashes of the previous month began to replay in his mind. He wished he could go back in time and change it all.

Angelo and Kina sat at the edge of two medical beds in a small office. With their sleeves pulled up over their elbows and a nurse holding an alcohol pad and needle, they playfully argued over who would be first. They knew the prick of the needle would sting their skin but they were too happy to be afraid or nervous about it.

"Ladies first of course," Angelo joked.

"Fine. I'll take it like a man for you," Kina joked back. She extended her arm for the nurse to grab. The nurse tapped on the veins in the center of her arm before wiping the area clean with an alcohol swab. Kina shrieked and Angelo cowered away by dropping his head and covering his eyes.

"They say that marriage can be painful at times," he joked. He held out his arm for the nurse to grab.

"You two are getting married? How sweet" The nurse commented.

"Yeah. This is the final stage. Once we find out we're not brother and sister, we good to go." Angelo said and Kina laughed.

The county they lived in required them to take a blood test to be sure they weren't related. Without it, they couldn't get their marriage license.

"Okay, well do you both want to test for HIV and AIDs also?"

Angelo and Kina smiles faded from their faces. Kina rolled down her sleeve in a nervous reaction and Angelo's knee jerked. All they wanted to do was get married. Not think about HIV. When they finally mustered up enough courage to make eye contact with each other, they stared back at each other quizzically as if the nurse's question was something they never considered. Neither one of them was sick. They barely had a common cold in the five years they had been together. Surely, they didn't have HIV. But, still, they felt uncomfortable discussing it.

"Um…we just wanted to get this out of the way so we can be married." Angelo made an excuse. Kina looked relieved as she nodded in agreement.

"It won't be any extra time or require any more blood. You can get the results back at the same time. It's up to you though," the nurse subtly pressured them. "So do you want me to mark that here as well?"

Angelo felt trapped and Kina was mute. They had no reason to say no yet the awkwardness lingered in their eyes. The nurse placed the notepad under Angelo's nose and he somehow nodded yes and signed the form. Kina fell in line.

"Great. I'll mail the results to the address listed," she said before leaving the room. The air in the room grew thick. They poked around at their bandages all the while avoiding eye contact with one another.

"Does it hurt?" Angelo asked.

He wanted to break the ice with small chat. This day was supposed to be special. He didn't want to ruin the mood.

"Not really. Yours?"

"It's okay."

"Was that appropriate?" Kina finally asked.

"What?" Angelo responded but he knew what she meant.

"The nurse kind of pressuring us to test," Kina answered.

"I didn't feel pressured cause I know I don't have anything to worry about." He slid off the table.

"Me either," Kina added and smoothed out the wrinkles in her shirt.

"You really shouldn't. You definitely don't look sick or thin. All that you got back there." He playfully smacked her butt. "And look at me. I work out every day." Angelo flexed his bulging biceps. "And I went a whole two years without getting a simple cold. I'm as healthy as an ox and more energetic than a man half my age. You of all people should know that," he flirted with Kina.

"I know. I'm not worried. I just didn't feel that it was appropriate. How she asked us and all. Besides, I know people with the bug and there's little ways you can tell. Especially with black folks. Your hair texture changes, you'd be having them dark circles around your eyes and under your neck. I even heard that when you're getting your hair permed, for some reason if you got it the perm changes colors. Something to do with the chemicals."

Kina recited folktales to ease the tension but deep down inside, they both knew they indulged in unprotected sex and that was the only way, aside from being a drug user, that you got the virus.

"I don't know bout all that but I know that we straight. I got tested, what?" he raised his head in the air, "three years ago and you..."

"Two years ago," she quickly interjected like that meant something.

"So whatever. We just better pray we ain't brother and sister. Then we gone really have some problems." Kina smiled and wrapped her arms around Angelo's neck, planting a kiss on his lips. And that was that. They didn't think about it again. Not even once.

"I can't wait to marry you," Kina said to Angelo.

"And I can't wait to marry you," Angelo responded.

THE SHARP EDGES of the small plastic squares, prickled against his cheek. Angelo looked up. Kina was shoving her hand in a cardboard box and pulling out condoms to throw at him. "I made my effort. See...all these damn condoms I bought. I took time to buy them. Not you. Me," she pounded on her chest. "Had me looking like a whore in Walmart because you didn't want to wear them," she complained. "Extra large…super…" she read the box. "Magnium, Lifestyle, Trojan. None of them were ever right. Too tight. It's cutting off my blood circulation. They were all too tight.

"Well, I hate to break it to you but you aint that big!!" She yelled. "If it wasn't too tight it was too dry, too phony feeling. Yet, I kept going out my way trying to find the perrrrrrfect condom for you. Like a damn Goldie Locks. Yep, that's exactly what I am. Goldie Locks and you the Big Bad Wolf here to kill me." She threw the empty box at him before rushing back to her room to pull out more.

"My, what a big ego you have…my, what big penis you have…" she mocked the fairy tale adding her remix. "Go ahead, Angelo. Say your part. It's better to kill you with my darling." She ripped open the second box and continued to throw the condoms at him. "You just feel so good baby," she imitated Angelo's voice. "I don't want nothing to separate our love. A rubber will separate us. I want to get closer to you," Kina huffed. "And I actually fell for the shit," she scoffed. "I want to experience the real you." Kina's sorrow turned to anger. She threw the last box at Angelo. The corner bounced of his head. "You probably did this to me on purpose. You just wanted to trap me. You jealous of me and my family, always been. That's why you don't want to let me go! Because you have no one!"

"Jealous!" Angelo jumped up. He brought himself out of his comatose state. "On purpose? Are you serious?" he screamed. He grabbed Kina by her forearms and shook her while yelling, "THIS AINT MY FAULT. IT AINT MY FAULT."

Kina pushed him off.

"I trapped you? Why the fuck would I do that? I can have any woman I want. Talking bout you gave me five grand for my car. I didn't want the damn car. You wanted me to have it. Always trying to make me something I'm not. You and your bougie family. You offered to drive my mamma to the doctor and you damn near begged my little sister to move in. You think I didn't know what you were doing? You the one that tried to trap me and you didn't mind me not wearing condoms. You the one that said you think you were allergic to them!"

"I tried to get you to use the lamb skin," Kina defended herself. She didn't like the way Angelo was fighting back.

"All that shopping and not one of these damn condoms is lamb skin." He picked a handful of condoms up from the floor and threw them back at Kina. "'It do feel better, Angelo,' you said." He mocked her. "You sure didn't put a fight whenever I would go in raw. You didn't even try. You just bought the damn condoms to clear your conscience. That's all they were for. Not protection."

"I said that once," Kina yelled back. "Once, I told you that I felt better without it but that didn't mean I had to have it without."

"Well, I didn't force you to do nothing you didn't want to do."

"You the one been running around with all these women!"

"Yeah and you chose to forgive me every time. I don't ever remember coming back here on my hand and knees begging you to stay with me. You knew I wasn't ready." Angelo waved his hands in the air. "Yet, you kept me around. Forgiving me. Waiting on me to be ready and now you want to blame me? You say I tried to trap you? You got me fucked up? You tried to trap me." He stabbed himself in the chest with his finger. "Trying to get in good with my family so they can pressure me to marry you like they did. You knew what I was out there doing. Everybody did. And who said it was me that did this? It could be you?"

"Me!" she yelled. "How dare you?" She charged towards him but he dodged her blow. Kina plunged head first into the couch cushion and punched the couch instead.

"You the only one I slept with unprotected. Not those other women. You think I'm crazy? I don't wear condoms with you because I trust you and I thought you trusted me. It was our thing. Something we could have together and it made it special. I ain't never been swimming in no other woman swamp without wearing my swimsuit. Never!"

"You a lie. What about Tasha?" Angelo looked away. "Yeah. How y'all have that baby? In Vitro?"

"That was one slip up and me and Tasha both been tested since then."

"You sure it was once?" Kina asked, sarcastic. "Everybody knows the situation with her and her man."

"That man aint gay. It's a rumor."

"I seen him out with a guy with my own eyes, Angelo!" Angelo continuously shook his head in disagreement. He didn't want to believe Kina but he heard the rumors himself and he did have another slip up with Tasha. It was on Christmas Eve night. Nothing planned, it just happened. He made an effort to spend every Christmas Eve with his son. It was last Christmas Eve, he didn't know if it was the Christmas spirit in the air, the spiked eggnog or the feeling of being with the mother of his child on such a special holiday that motivated their "slip up", nevertheless it happened.

ANGELO HAD JUST taken the last swallow of his fourth cup of eggnog. Tasha was on her third. Every sip after his fourth cup caused his head to get heavy and his spirit lighter. His three-year-old son lay on a pillow on top of the couch. Whitney Houston's voice trailed out from the small speakers, singing the tunes of Silent Night. The dim lights from the Christmas tree colorfully lit up the living room and the smell of wood burning on the fireplace gave Angelo a warm and fuzzy feeling. He had a glimpse of how real family life would be. A thought of Kina flashed through his mind but he took another sip of eggnog and the image of her began to vanish.

Tasha's boyfriend was back in jail. He wasn't going to be released until after the holidays and she was growing fed up with his antics. Angelo and Tasha tried to keep their relationship platonic but there was something about that night that made it hard. Tasha lay across the couch next to their son and he sat on the ground but somewhere in between his fifth glass and her fourth glass, they sat side by side. Her bare thigh pressed against his jeans. They shared laughs and exchanged sorrows. Soft, brief touches became long, gentle caresses and before Whitney hummed her last tune, they were giving each other heavy kisses. They didn't pace themselves, but jumped right into action. Tasha's flirty nightie made this easy. By the time he pressed his weight on top of her body, he knew to ask before it went any further.

"Wait a minute, wait. You know what we need to do. Remember," he pointed to his sleeping son. A physical reminder of the risk of not using condoms. They were only worried about bearing more children. They didn't consider anything else. Besides, they had been there once before. Having sex without condoms after the first time was easy. Tasha smiled.

"Follow me." Angelo followed her to the bedroom. He lay across the bed with his head spinning. When Tasha returned, she had an oops look on her face and was empty-handed.

"What you got for me?" He referred to the condom.

"It's on you," she replied while climbing back into bed. They jumped right back where they left off; this time even quicker. As their hormones reached an all-time high, he whispered softly in her ear,

"I aint got nothing." Tasha didn't respond or offer him the same verbal disclosure but Angelo didn't need her to.

"YOU JUST SEEING what you want to see. Just like you trying to make this whole situation my fault and it aint!! It aint!! I can't take this blame. I'm not at fault."

"What you mean it's not your fault? This is all on you. I've been faithful to you since day one. I haven't even as much as looked at another man since I've been with you. Waiting on you to settle. I hoped that you would get it all out of your system. Apparently I was wrong cause not only is it never going to get out of your system, it's attached itself to mine! I've been good to you, Angelo. I don't sleep around, I haven't had that many sexual partners. This aint fair. I don't deserve this," Kina sobbed.

"Oh, so you perfect now? You forgetting where I met you?"

"It was a joke. I was in that strip club with my friends as a joke. We were just clowning around."

"You calling me a liar? Acting like you're little miss goody two shoes and you admitted to me you stepped out on your ex Jacob and Franko…"

"I was 16 when I was with Jacob and 18 when I was with Franko."

"You forgetting Rodney?" Kina quickly looked away. She did forget Rodney. She had pushed that mistake far out of her mind because he wasn't supposed to happen. "Oh, you aint got no chat back now huh? Thought I forgot about Hot Rod. You told me yourself. Remember. Talking about you tired of me messing around on you and you gone pay me back. So this is what you do huh? Tell me the details. I want to hear them now." Kina remained silent. "Go ahead, tell me. When it happened you damn near broke your neck trying to tell me what y'all did. I WANT TO HEAR IT NOW." He yelled. Kina turned to walk away but Angelo pulled her back. "Tell me."

"I was safe!" she cried out. "I was…" Kina buried her face in her hands and sobbed. Her intentions were to be safe that night but Rodney had a different plan.

"Where is it?" Kina searched in between the sheets. Rodney rested his head on a pillow and lit a cigarette. He was unmoved by Kina's frantic state of mind. "Rodney, don't play with me."

"I thought that's what you wanted," he said in between puffs. "To play games." Kina got down on all fours and searched under the bed and around the floor. "Telling me all that stuff about your man. You wanted me to be your one night wonder to help you forget him and that's what I was. I had fun. You didn't?"

"Where's the damn rubber, Rodney?" Kina looked up.

"What rubber?" Rodney smirked.

"The one I gave you to put on."

"You wanted me to put that on," he chuckled.

Kina sighed. "You a bastard for this. Why the hell you think I gave it to you? You being spiteful."

"Why you tripping? When we ever used rubbers before?"

"You aint my man, Rodney and haven't been for years now. What right do you think you have to do that?"

"Seemed like you was enjoying it to me. You know the difference between paper and plastic. Don't nothing plastic feel that real."

"I didn't know," Kina defended herself.

"Stop tripping, you knew. What? You worried I gave you a baby? Hope I did."

"Don't say that." She slapped him across the chest. "You the last man I want a baby with."

"Your man stepped out and got him one. I thought this was payback? You don't know how to play the game."

"Rodney, I aint been with you like that for a while now. I don't know what you been up to."

"I been locked up for five years girl. Can't go no safer than me. Nobody in that cage but me, myself, and I. Now if you can contract something by choking and jerking, then we in problems otherwise stop tripping."

"I hear about what happens to you men in prison." Kina replied. Rodney jumped up. He was no longer smirking.

"What you trying to say, I aint no man?"

"I just hear stuff," Kina responded.

"Hear stuff from who? From where? TV? Stop watching so many damn movies!" Rodney yelled. He lit his cigarette out on her sheets before leaning over towards the night stand and pulling out the unopened condom from underneath the lamp. "Here's your damn rubber," he threw it at her before pulling on his jeans.

⁓

"RODNEY WAS ONCE and it was because of you," she deflected.

"Well, I hope it was to die for," he said, sarcastic. "Y'all woman stupid. At least I'm careful with mine. Y'all want somebody to fulfill your fantasies," he threw up his arms. "Sleeping with these ex-cons thinking it's gone be so great forgetting about what really goes on there."

"That only happens on TV. That don't happen in real life. They the safest men on earth." Kina said hopefully, repeating what Rodney told her.

"Ha," Angelo bent over slapping his leg, laughing and full of anger, "did you really say what I think you said? Did you?" He was sarcastic. "And you blaming me? You real clever, Kina. Always have been." He walked over to her and leaned in close. His nose almost touching the tip of her nose. "Clever as hell," he repeated. "Talking about I did this on purpose. You the one that was all nervous about taking the test. If it wasn't for me suggesting it, we would have never took it."

"You didn't suggest anything; you were forced to do it. Maybe you wanted to get your secret out."

"You could have already had the results," he picked up the crumbled test results and carefully smoothed the wrinkles out the paper. "Maybe you been planning these outburst so that you can take the blame off yourself. Maybe you been with Rodney more than once. You sneaky." He threw the paper at her face.

"I didn't know. I was actually excited when they came. I wasn't thinking about tricking you. I was thinking that we could apply for a marriage license, finalize with the pastor, and get married! It's all I was thinking. That's all. Since we took the test it's all I've been thinking about. Never this! I didn't expect this. I didn't plan this and I wouldn't wish this on my enemy. I just wanted to get the marriage licenses that's it," Kina's body fell to the ground. She sobbed at Angelo's feet. She never fathomed the test would come back that they were both HIV positive. Especially at 30 years old; the unthinkable happened which was just as rare and random to them as a piano falling out the sky. A few hours earlier she was making breakfast and humming in the kitchen. Now this.

IT WAS ONE of those calm Sunday mornings where the cold winter months was coming to an end and spring was peeking through the air, revealing itself through the colorful blossoming flowers and occasional warm breeze. Everything felt new. Kina sifted through the mail while Angelo lay across the couch laughing heartily at a comical movie. The stack of mail, that sat in a clumsy pile on the dining room table for weeks, consisted of bridal magazines, light bill, credit card statements, and a letter addressed to her and Angelo from the Shelton Medical Clinic.

"Oh, good. It finally came. Now we can apply for the license and get the pastor." Kina said to herself. She did a little dance as she slit the envelope open with her finger nail. She pulled out a white letter with the clinic's letter head and a yellow carbon copy printed with red ink. She skipped the letter and skimmed through the carbon copy. It all looked foreign to her. A bunch of numbers mixed with alphabets and percentages. Then she saw Angelo's last name and beside it was positive. Her last name shared the identical marking of positive. Her heart raced. It felt like it was going to fracture her chest yet she kept her composure.

She studied the paper further but her fear crippled her ability to concentrate. Her hands shook so uncontrollably the paper rattled. Angelo yelled something to her from the couch but she didn't pay him any attention; the letter was so loud it silenced his voice. Her knees felt weak and her stomach went sour. She swallowed hard to keep herself from pushing up the breakfast of bacon and pancakes she had a few hours prior. Kina pushed the yellow carbon copy to the side and read the letter. It was in a language she could understand. The words HIV and positive where highlighted in bold writing. Then her eyes landed on the words 'we regret to inform you'. The last thing she saw was a 1-800 number she could call for help. Who could help them now? She thought to herself. Not even God could help them. It was too late.

Her body fell back. She clutched on to the laminate countertop to hold up her weight. She felt as if she had died. She had always wondered what death felt like, now she knew. Her chest continued to heave in and out and her heavy breathing reduced to desperate panting. She felt like she was hyperventilating. Kina tripped over the trash can. She suddenly had the urge to get rid of it; make it all go away. She would stuff the letter way down in the bottom of the bag and make herself forget. What Angelo didn't know wouldn't hurt and what the letter was alleging could never be true. At least not in her world.

Kina dangled the papers over the trash. She shook them but it was if they were glued to her fingertips she couldn't let them go. It didn't matter if she threw the paper away, it would always be there and in her mind. Somehow, she made her way to the living room where Angelo lay. She stumbled in front of him holding out the yellow paper in front of her like it was their death sentence. Angelo looked at her quizzically. Then Kina mumbled out, "We're positive."

SEEING KINA IN pain reminded Angelo of how much he loved her. And he knew she loved him. They loved each other and love was going to get them through this regardless of who was at fault. Angelo leaned over and grabbed Kina by her arms, pulling her up from the ground. Kina slid down his chest. She was too weak to stand. Angelo knew he had to be her strength and she would have to be his. They were in this together.

"It's not my fault, Angelo. It's not," she mumbled in between sobs.

"It's not mine either," he whispered loudly.

"Then who?!" Kina yelled. "Who?" Angelo squeezed Kina's squirming body. He held her until she squirmed no more.

"It doesn't matter now." He kissed the top of her head and cried silent tears. "We are going to get through this like no one's at fault."

The End

Three Reasons Why

~~⌒⌒⌒~~

CYNTHIA SAT ON the toilet and stared down at the single blue line, long and hard. She closed her eyes tightly and said a silent prayer then reopened them only to find the same single blue line. She wasn't pregnant. She remembered back to a time where she prayed to see the blue line. It was ironic how things worked out.

~~⌒⌒⌒~~

(The First Reason Why)

CYNTHIA FELT SOMEONE pressing down on her mattress. It interrupted her afterschool nap. She looked up to find her aunt, holding the bathroom trashcan over her head. She lowered it and shook the trashcan, making sure that Cynthia saw what was in it. Cynthia wondered what she had done this time. Did she throw away the toothpaste before it was all gone? Did she use too much paper towel for drying her hands? With her aunt being a nagging impossible clean freak, it could have been anything. Cynthia looked down in the trash can. It was nothing there but hand napkins and tissue balls.

"You get a good look because I did," her aunt continued to shake the trashcan in her face.

"What I do?" Cynthia replied, confused. She leaned up and wiped the sleep from her face.

"That's my point exactly. What have you been doing, child?" She slammed the trashcan down and lifted Cynthia off the bed by her forearm.

"Ouch," Cynthia hollered. "What I do? I didn't do nothing."

"Stay here," she yelled back at Cynthia. Cynthia folded her arms into her chest and rolled her eyes at her aunt's back. Her aunt returned holding a calendar and a small bag. She squinted her eyes scornfully at Cynthia. "What month are we in, child?"

"What you mean?" Cynthia snapped. Her aunt grabbed her by the arm and shook her.

"Girl, don't give me no attitude. What month are we in?"

"March," Cynthia answered. She didn't know where her aunt was going with this. Her aunt flipped the calendar back two pages.

"What month is this?" She pointed down on the bold lettering. Cynthia gave her aunt attitude by sucking her teeth and huffing her breath before answering,

"It's January, Auntie."

"January," she repeated and moved in closer to Cynthia. She lifted up the trashcan again and pushed it into her chest. "For two months I've been watching this can," she referred to the trash. "It ain't been nothing in it. When's the last time you had your monthly?"

"My monthly?" Cynthia was still confused.

"Your cycle, child."

Embarrassed by her aunt's forwardness, she looked away.

Her aunt grabbed her chin and turned her head back to face her. "You been sinning in my house?"

"No," she answered quickly.

"Yes, you have. I've seen you with them neighborhood boys. I seen you trying to corrupt those boys in your uncle's church. You got you a Jezebel

spirit on you. Just like your mamma. Same unclean curse," her tone was cold. Her words were so harsh, Cynthia's chest burned. She hated when her aunt talked about her mother; the mother she never met.

Cynthia's mother had her at 16 but died during childbirth. Complications that even as an adult she would never understand. She bounced around from aunt to aunt but spent the last five years of her 15 years of living with her great aunt Marsha and her pastor husband. Cynthia hated staying with her. She was the worst kind of Christian. Judgmental, hypocritical, and overly religious.

Her aunt pulled out a cardboard box from the bag she carried in her room; it was a pregnancy test. "You go in that bathroom and read these direction and you better do it right. I'll be waiting right here when you get out and you better pray for God's mercy, child." She pushed Cynthia in the direction of the bathroom. Cynthia had never taken a pregnancy test before. She had never even considered pregnancy before this day. Her mind was still that of a child, a sheltered child, and it dwelled on childish things. Cynthia didn't know anything about sex or safe sex for that matter; only the basics and what she saw on TV. Her aunt never sat her down and had the talk with her. All Cynthia knew about sex from her aunt was that it was evil. In her aunt's house, the concept of sex and sexuality was like the elephant in the room that everyone pretended not to notice; until now.

Cynthia stared down at the box. Although she was alone, she felt so ashamed. She avoided looking at her reflection in the mirror. It didn't feel right for her to be peeing on a plastic stick and then handing over the results to her aunt. Cynthia was a private person. When she first started her period, she hid it from her aunt for months until she found out by searching through the trash. Starting her period was the official mark of her womanhood and she wasn't ready for that; she had no example on what a woman should be and feared that she wasn't prepared for it. So she ignored it and what it meant. Her period was the sign that her time as a child was up and she wasn't ready for that.

Her aunt banged on the door yelling for her to hurry up. "Child, don't make me have to come in there and administer the results in person." It didn't take as long as the box explained. As soon as Cynthia wet the stick, the two lines appeared in the white window box. They were faint, but bold enough for Cynthia to understand. She was pregnant.

"Give me that," her aunt snatched the plastic applicator out of her hand. "Oh, lawd!" she screamed like she had just received a death sentence. "I knew it. I just knew it!" she yelled up to the ceiling. Cynthia knew that she was gesturing to God. "Why? Oh, why? Has she come to destroy us?" She grabbed Cynthia and pushed her back into her bedroom. "Get on your knees and pray for forgiveness."

"Auntie, I…I," Cynthia was in shock.

"Get down." She pushed down on her shoulders until Cynthia was on her knees. She waved her Bible over Cynthia's head. Cynthia cried. She was scared and embarrassed; she felt unclean. "I knew the second that I brought you in this house you was going to be trouble. Just like your mamma. Running around dealing with men like some hoemonger. I knew it. How dare you disrespect me and the pastor in our own house? We brought you in when you had nowhere to go and you bring your sinful ways in our home. You open the door for all the evil spirits to come in and dwell in our holy home," She raised her hand and slapped Cynthia's jaw; the smack echoed but it didn't hurt as much as her words. "You're going to have to answer to God for your sinful ways. Just like your mamma."

"I'm sorry, Auntie."

"Don't you dare apologize to me. Apologize to the lawd. He's the one that has to forgive you. All these women out here. These good, holy, married women that can't give their husbands children and you running around taking advantage of the gift that God gave you. How many little boys you been with? Huh? How many?"

Cynthia answered with heavy sobs.

"Just one, Auntie." She grabbed Cynthia by her shirt's collar.

"Don't lie to me."

"I swear. Just one. I didn't know…I didn't know that we did it…"

"You're a liar." She slapped her again. "A nasty liar."

"Just one," Cynthia screamed. "Just one."

Cynthia was telling the truth. The boy was really a man. At least to

Cynthia he was. He was her Aunt Marsha's twenty-year-old stepson, Malik and the only one person Cynthia thought her aunt hated more than her. The pastor had Malik a year before he married Aunt Marsha. Malik was a constant reminder of what she couldn't give her husband, a child.

He didn't come around much; Aunt Marsha would make up excuses as to why he couldn't visit. But when he was around, he was the only one that paid Cynthia any attention. He was like her mother, her father, and her companion all in one. He told her how pretty she was, how smart she was, and how proud he was of her for not being like the rest of the girls her age. Then one day out of nowhere, he kissed her; one kiss. The gateway to this day. Her first kiss turned into her first feel as Malik slipped his hand into the opening of her shirt. Then it became the first time a boy had ever touched her below the belt. Cynthia didn't know what to expect and she grew curious about his next move; she anticipated how it would make her feel. So, she didn't object when he slipped off her underwear and climbed on top of her. When they were done, it was so quick that she didn't know if she had gone all the way or not. It throbbed and burned down there but what he did didn't make her moan like the women on T.V so she just assumed she didn't have sex. Therefore, she had to still be a virgin. And virgins didn't get pregnant. Cynthia knew that much. However, the plastic test showed otherwise. Afterwards, their relationship went back to normal. It was almost like it never happened and pretty soon Cynthia had almost forgotten herself.

Aunt Marsha started to hit Cynthia with the Bible. Envy lurked behind her angry eyes. Cynthia pleaded with her to stop, she felt like the devil himself. "You gone tell me who. I want to know who you corrupted." Cynthia knew she couldn't tell. She wouldn't believe her. The pastor's son wasn't capable of such evil. Her aunt finally tired herself out. She let the Bible fall down onto the floor beside Cynthia and prayed to God to help her catch her breath. "Lord, this child is trying to kill me," she said in between huffs. "You're not going to mention a word of this to the pastor. Not one word. I'm going to fix this. You better be glad I got enough mercy not to throw you back out on the streets."

"Fix it?" Cynthia was naïve.

"Fix it. Trust me, you gone thank me for this one day. You're going to

thank me." She repeated through heavy breathing. "If you ever mention this to the pastor or anybody, God is going to rain His wrath down on you," she threatened Cynthia. It was a Friday afternoon when Cynthia found out that she was pregnant and by Monday morning, she was counting backwards from one hundred on a cold steel table. Everything happened so quick, Cynthia didn't have time to digest what happened.

CYNTHIA PLACED THE negative pregnancy test on the sink before washing her hands. The floor creaked outside the door as the steps from the other end continued to pace back and forth, anxious yet hopeful. When the moving outside the door stopped, the taps began. It was the same routine as the last three times; almost identical. Same single blue line, same anxious pacing outside the door and, most of all, the same heart-wrenching disappointment that weighed down her chest.

The first tap on the door was more like a knock as it was always louder than the ones that would soon follow. Using all four knuckles, Daniel knocked on the door loud enough for her to hear. It was his way of letting her know that he could no longer wait for the results. When there was no response, his knock fiddled down into light taps. So faint that if she wasn't listening, she would have missed them. It was his disappointed tap. His acceptance tap. Then the third and final tap came. This was what she considered to be the warning tap. She knew he was going to enter the bathroom. The warning tap gave them both time to correct the disappointment that slumped in their shoulders and weighed down their necks into false hope. "You okay in there?" Daniel asked as usual. He cracked open the door and stuck his head in first. He forced a smile on his face. His mouth could lie with a false curve of lips but his eyes always told the truth. Cynthia held up the long white stick and said,

"Blue."

"How many blue?" He held his faith to the end.

Cynthia had told him before that positive would show two red lines not two blues, just one blue for negative. He knew how it worked because he saw the explanations on the commercials that always popped up and left an awkward mood in the room, he studied the same box, reading the directions once every month for the past three months when she flashed the stick in his face but still he asked. Cynthia held up her index finger and gestured the response, "one."

"Oh," he looked down on the floor, "okay," he said and darted his eyes back in her direction. He didn't want them to linger away too long. He wanted her to know that he was pretending to be hopeful.

"This has to be a sign. We keep getting blue so that must mean that it's going to be a boy when it finally turns red," Cynthia lied to him with her smile. "Two reds," she gestured again with her fingers. She always knew just what to say to him to lift his mood. Daniel's faith was something he took serious as he lived off optimism and all the *what-ifs* the world had to offer as an alternative to accepting the truth and allowing himself to feel the disappointment that came with reality.

"You're right. We have to be aware of the signs. I mean, we need to prepare because I'm feeling a boy too."

"But most of all Daniel, we have to be patient."

"Of course, there's no rush," he lied and walked out the bathroom. Cynthia followed behind him. He started to pace again. "I mean you're only 30. I know they say you should try to have all your kids before 34 because it decreases risk but I know that's not going to be our case."

Cynthia read between the lines. It was Daniel's way of indirectly letting her know that her biological clock was ticking and if she didn't have a baby soon, her time with him would be out. "And some say it gets harder every year after thirty but, that can't be true for everybody." He hid his condescending tone behind a smile. In his mind, she was the reason they couldn't conceive because he was too perfect to be incapable of doing what everybody else in his circle was doing. "We can wait."

"Or, we can just try again," she put her hands on his shoulder. She wanted a child too but not as bad as him. She knew that having the baby would not only give her another 10-15 years in their marriage but also be a lucrative exit plan if things didn't work out. Daniel provided Cynthia with a lifestyle that she grew accustomed to. All she had to do was workout, eat right, stay fit and pretty, and make a baby or two and she would be able to keep the riches he offered to her.

A baby would complete their perfect family just like adding the 13 light crystal chandelier completed their dining room. It was all for show. The Facebook post. The Christmas cards. The pictures Daniel would hang in the office. The conversations he would be a part of at work. Little versions of him walking and talking and making him proud became an obsession. He had to have a baby.

Six months into the marriage and they were having the baby conversation. He planned it so that during their third year of marriage they would start preparing to conceive. He figured that would be enough time for them to vacation and take long weekends so that they didn't feel like they missed out on anything. Besides, anything sooner than that would be taboo in Daniel's world. Three years in was perfect timing for a baby. He was so sure that when he was ready it would happen just like everything else in his life. His life was privileged that way.

He was a classic Type A personality and a die-hard perfectionist. Cynthia hid her imperfections from him with her beauty; it was easier for Cynthia to look perfect than to be perfect and in reality, Daniel preferred it that way. Cleaning up pretty hid the dirt from Cynthia's past.

Perfection meant everything to Daniel. Everything in his life was timed and organized exactly how he planned it. He was a firm believer in being in control of his destiny. To Daniel, obstacles weren't things in the way of what he wanted but simply things to step over or kick when necessary. Cynthia admired him for his way of thinking although it intimidated her.

To outsiders looking in, Daniel had it all; the perfectly landscaped 4000 square foot house, the shiny black Mercedes, and the elegant and beautiful stay at home wife; a woman beautiful enough for him to prance around his business associates and friends, and educated enough to hold a conversation. He loved how they admired her beauty out of the corner of their eyes and how distracted they became whenever she was around; she completed him.

Image was even more important to him than money. Daniel came from money and not new money but money that could be traced back three generations. His great grandfather was a bootlegger, after the prohibition he had a head start. He cleaned his money and took his name and turned it into a brand that covered the labels of the highest quality whiskey. Most of his thinking and steadfast business ways were inherited by his father and grandfather. He was under a lot of pressure to outdo his father the same way his father outdid his grandfather. Financially, he was reaching his goal but his family life needed work. His obsession was taking over him. He wanted to stamp his mark on the world just like his father and grandfather had done. So that even after he was long gone, somehow he still would be here. Without children, he felt that all his hard work would be in vain. And it made him feel like he was less of a man. His father always said that you weren't truly a man until you fathered children.

Cynthia knew that in his own way he loved her, but not enough to stay with her without children; that had nothing to do with love. It was where his love and nature parted ways. If Cynthia didn't produce children for him within in a year, he would simply replace her like he did his Benz, for a newer efficient model.

Daniel was Cynthia's security. Her retirement plan. And her beloved seat at the table with the elites. Daniel introduced her into a lifestyle she didn't believe existed beyond T.V screens. She didn't grow up with a mother or a father. He sold her on the image of family; something that was no more than an adolescent fantasy to her. But she knew well enough to understand that their marriage was a business deal too. It had to fit into his model.

"I printed some more information off the net for you to read," He gestured to their nightstand. It was a stack of papers sitting on top of a book called *The Craftiness of Conception,* a book she read from cover to cover in less than 24 hours. She studied the book like she had a test in the morning.

"Okay, I'll skim through it later tonight."

"You might want to take notes. Some of that stuff is real intense. I heard it was really helpful."

Cynthia cracked a slight smile and pretended to be interested in the research he found. The truth was she had grown tired of him and his get pregnant quick remedies. After every negative test, came another method. Each one more bogus than the next.

"Head stands," she said with a raised brow.

"Yeah," He leaned over her shoulder and began to point at the drawings to further explain. "You see it's one of those ancient Egyptian methods. You do it during the first full moon."

"I heard of this. You know Kiza, my stylist, she suggested this to me. I thought it was silly."

"Kiza?" his tone changed. He cleared his throat. "Cynthia, I thought that we were going to be discreet about this. We don't want people out there thinking we're having trouble with this."

Nothing could be worse to Daniel than people assuming they were barren. The thought sickened Daniel. All the books he ordered on conception he had them shipped. He never picked them up in person from a bookstore. Daniel didn't have to worry about Kiza though. She was the only one that Cynthia confided. She vented to Kiza about all her fears of not being able to conceive and told her that she thought they were having problems because of the three abortions she had before she met Daniel. Kiza gave her the book to ease her mind. She told her that it wasn't true because she had done two abortions and still was able to have three kids. Kiza was the only one she could talk to about this because the very conservative, opinionative, and judgmental Daniel would never understand.

She turned to face him. "I've been discreet," she cupped his face with her hands and gave him a soft kiss on his lips. "She mentioned it to me first. She just assumed that we would be trying to have children by now."

"Well, it's not her business."

"You're right, Daniel. I'm sorry."

"It's okay. Don't get stressed out," he said quickly. "You need to relax," he massaged her shoulders although he needed the massage more. "We're going to have dinner at mom's with the rest of the family and really enjoy ourselves tonight. No baby worries," he convinced himself. "Patience," he raised his index finger. "It's the key to it all. Patience."

~~~

CYNTHIA SAT AT the long marble dining table. All the seats of the table, that sat 12, were occupied by Daniel's siblings and their children. One Sunday a month, his mother will cater a family dinner. It was a tradition that Cynthia learned to enjoy. Daniel's mother was the mother she never had; she was almost perfect. A beautiful socialite, full of wit, wisdom, and wealth. Even with all her money, she was the kind of down to earth woman that wasn't afraid to be herself. In turn, Cynthia felt like she could be herself around her; even more so than when she was around Daniel. Cynthia watched Daniel's sister in-laws as they cradled their newborns in their arms while their husbands bounced their toddlers on their knees. Whenever one of the children would call out, *Daddy*, Daniel took a long sip of his Chardonnay and swallowed hard. Being a naturally competitive person, the fact that he was the oldest child with no children of his own killed him. Both his brothers were ahead of him by two and half.

"Well…are you two going to make me wait or do you have something to share with us?" Daniel's mother pried. She smiled wide and hopeful; she was where Daniel inherited his undying faith. Daniel cleared his throat. He washed down his embarrassment with another long sip of Chardonnay. Cynthia shook her head, no at his mother. His mother frowned briefly before pepping back up. "It's okay, honey. You know what they say," she held up her wine glass, "third time is the charm. Let's toast to Daniel and Cynthia." They held up their wine glasses.

"Here, here," his brother Rodger said in a condescending tone.

"But isn't this in fact," he paused, "the third time?" he held up three fingers.

"Yes, Rodger. But that doesn't bother me at all," Daniel lied. "Let any great business man tell you their story and he'll tell you how many times he failed before excelling," he said wearing one of his phony salesman smiles. "Failure is almost one of the most important parts of success."

Cynthia was uncomfortable with Daniel using the word failure; it was almost if he was indirectly referring to her.

"Shut up, Rodger. Third time, fourth time. These things just take time," Daniel's mother interrupted. "Getting pregnant is not as easy as you would think." Cynthia forced on a worry free smile to assure his mom her encouraging words were enough to keep her motivated. However, Cynthia knew from her own experience that getting pregnant could be that easy; in fact, almost effortless. Her mind drifted off to the second time she accidently got pregnant.

～

(The second reason why)

CYNTHIA LAY ACROSS the bed face down and sobbed hard into a pillow. The pillow's soft cushion soaked in her tears while silencing the sounds of her loud cry. She squeezed on tight to the cordless phone before hammering it into the mattress. She pounded the phone against the bed until her arm grew tired; this didn't make her feel better, so she did what she thought would. She rolled over on her back and sniffed in her tears. She slowly dialed the number; her hands trembled as she punched the keys. The phone rang five times before she got the voicemail. It used to ring three times before he picked up.

"Manny," she cried into the phone. It was her tenth time calling him that day. "Why are you doing this to me? I don't understand? I would never betray you. I didn't do this on purpose. I thought it was what you wanted, what we both wanted. I love you Manny. I need you. Please!" she screamed, "pick up the phone. It's been a week and you just abandon us like this. Like *we're nothing. I'll do whatever you want; Manny I just need to hear your voice. That's all," she sobbed.*

"I just need to hear your voice," she repeated again before ending the call. She screamed out and cried again but no tears came down. She was all cried out as her eyes burned and the hairs on her lashes felt tender against the lid. She placed her hands on her stomach and rubbed it in a circular motion. "I don't want to do this again," she said to herself. "I can't do this again. I won't." She raised her legs and kicked and pounded against the mattress with her fist; she acted out a temper tantrum. Cynthia flung her arms up and down until her body grew tired; soon after that, she dozed off.

When Cynthia heard her front door echo a knock, she thought that she was dreaming. When the knock became a bang, she leaned up. "Manny," she said to herself. She rushed to the bathroom before answering the door. She looked at her reflection in the mirror and frowned. Her hair lay flat and damp, from sweat and tears. It hung down her shoulders in a tangled ponytail. She pulled a brush out from a drawer. She brushed out as much freeze as she could. She splashed cold water on her face hopping that it reduced the puffiness that sat under her eyes. As the knocks continued, she adjusted her ratty night gown that she spent days in, and rushed to the door. She didn't waste any time looking through the peep hole or asking who was there; she flung open the door in a rush.

It wasn't Manny.

The woman stared back at Cynthia like she was a disease that she had the cure for. She had a key in the lock. She pulled it out after Cynthia opened the door and stuffed it in her designer bag. She rolled her eyes as if she were annoyed, and rested her hand on her very large belly. She looked as if she were due any day. The smell of her heavy scented perfume made Cynthia feel almost nauseous. "May I help you?" Cynthia played dumb.

"Yes, you can actually." She entered the apartment without Cynthia inviting her in. The woman walked through the door as if she owned the place. She placed her purse down on the stand and walked towards the couch. She brushed off lint from the seat's cushion before sitting. She searched every angle of the apartment with her eyes, as if she were inspecting it. Then she looked down at the coffee table; it didn't past her inspection. She sighed hard before adjusting the crystal vase and removing the metal

magazine rack. "This is a mahogany surface," she snapped. She licked her finger and cleaned away the almost unnoticeable marks the metal rack left.

"Why are you in my house?" Cynthia asked in a childish tone. The woman laughed before flipping her wavy hair.

"Your house?" she said, sarcastic. "You young girls really are a trip. You have warped reality when it comes to the things you think are yours."

"My fiancé and I live here together."

"Fiancé?" she was surprised. "Ha!" she clasped her hands together and leaned over to laugh. "I don't know if it's me getting older or you guys are getting dumber."

"No, I think you're just getting older," Cynthia snapped back. Cynthia's remark wiped the smirk off the woman's face.

"With age comes wisdom, little girl." She stared at Cynthia until Cynthia looked away. The woman intimidated her in every way. Her strength, her beauty, and her confidence. "You actresses really do live in a dream world." She leaned back and made herself comfortable on the couch. "You wouldn't know reality if you played the part on TV. Your fiancé, your little Hollywood apartment." She waved her arm in the air and shooed. "You young girls better wise up"

"Who are you? What do you want?"

"Child, don't play me. I may have retired from stage but I still and always will," she emphasized the word "always," "have the role of leading lady. You really think you gone come and take that from me?" she pointed from her chest. "Honey, you weren't the first little thing that thought they could fill my shoes and you won't be the last. I've been dealing with trifling little tricks like you for 10 years now. I'm an expert on your type. Young little aspiring starlets that think they can sleep their way up to the big screens"

"I love Manny. I don't have to do that for parts"

"You love my husband? You?" She leaned up from the couch. "You don't know love until you've been in it 10 years. Ten years of dealing with women like you. Cleaning all his mess, taking care of his kids."

"Kids?"

"Yes, sweetie. Kids. Three at home and one on the way." She pointed to her belly.

"Manny doesn't have kids. At least not yet." Cynthia grabbed her stomach. The woman rolled her eyes again. She leaned back on the couch. She was unmoved by Cynthia's gesture.

"Everybody wants to sleep with a Hollywood producer." She shook her head at Cynthia. "Manny Lee Productions. We built that together you know. It's a lot you don't know but so much you assume. You're a fool. You really think my husband is thinking about you. At the end of the day, it's business as usual for him. Now you done got yourself all knocked up, thinking you in love. There goes your career. Gone in a whim. Gone because some Hollywood producer told you that you had something special, that he loved you. If you knew anything about Manny you would know that he was an actor before he became a producer. He's always loved the art and what great actor he is. See how convinced he got you after only what four," she gestured the number with her hand, "or six months of being together. He played you just like he does all the rest. You see honey, this is the only role you ever were going to play for Manny. You spent six months calling it love when he spent six months playing make believe with you."

"No," Cynthia said while shaking her head.

"Believe it or not but it's over now."

"You're just here because you're jealous. He wants to leave you but…"

"Leave me? Honey, Manny will never leave me. You know why?" She paused. "Because I'm smarter than you. Because he needs me more than I'll ever need him and I designed it that way. Don't get it twisted. Yeah, he sleeps around but you don't think I know that? Who do you think got this apartment for him to put his little girls in? You or the rest of the world may not understand but it's our thing. He can have his girls on the side but he got his woman at home and to be honest I can care less. At least until they get knocked up. Then it's my business. Manny," she said while shaking her head. "I clean his mess in and out of home. If he don't start using condoms, I just might give him to you after all."

"I don't understand."

"You will one day but today just try and act," she gestured quotes with her fingers, *"like you understand."* She pulled an envelope out of her purse and handed it to Cynthia. Cynthia looked down at it like it was plagued. *"Fine,"* she placed it on the nightstand. *"You can read it later just let me give you a heads up. Inside is cash and directions to a very private clinic. The doctor is expecting your call."*

"Doctor for what?"

"Do I have to say it? This isn't a soap opera, sweetie. This doesn't have to be that dramatic. You're pregnant and my husband and I need you not to be. I can't force you to do it..."

"You sure can't," Cynthia interjected.

"But I can make your life a living hell for not doing it. You think you're going to get a dime from us? Well not without a fight. That bastard child in your stomach will be five years old before you see any cash and the only way he will ever see Manny is through TV screens and on magazine covers. And I'll make sure you never get work as an actress. The only TV you'll be doing is local commercials."

"You don't have the power."

"And you don't have a clue." Her tone went cold. *"And by the way, you're evicted as of today. I want you out. If you choose not to leave, I'll have the police escort you out. Please don't make me go through all that trouble. I have hair appointment that I can't be late for."* She stroked her hair. *"You know how impatient these Hollywood stylists can be."*

"I'm not leaving, signing or doing anything until I speak with Manny."

"Whatever," she sighed. She pulled out her cell phone and dialed the number. *"Manny. Hey baby it's me. I'm here, missing my appointment, handling your little situation. Un huh..."* she smiled. *"You better. Anyway she wants to talk with you. Make it quick because I got things to do,"* she handed Cynthia the phone.

"Hello," she whispered into the receiver. She walked back towards the bedroom so she could talk in private. The woman didn't object; she just sat on the couch and fiddled with her nails, unmoved.

"Manny. What's going on? I've been trying to call you all day. Where have you been?" she talked quickly.

"I've been at home with my wife and kids, Cent," he answered in a casual tone.

"Wife and kids. Kids? You told me…"

"I know what I told you, Cent. I thought we both knew this whole thing was a game. You know, just something to do for fun."

"What?"

"Come on, Cent. You know how the game is played and you know the rules. You broke the ultimate rule by getting pregnant. I don't want any part of that, babe."

"I didn't get pregnant on my own."

"We're not married, so you did get pregnant on your own."

"But you used to say that we would have a pretty child and we talked about what we would name our kids and…"

"Cent…Cent. You're going to have to calm down. Come on, Cent. You couldn't have thought that was true. Where did you think I went at night or in the morning? You never saw a picture of me and my wife and kids in a magazine? Come on, Cent, you knew the deal. You just thought that you could be an exception to the rules."

"No! I thought you loved me."

"I'm sorry if I misled you but kids," he paused, "that's going too far. I can't have a bunch of kids outside of my marriage. That's tacky and I won't do it. I suggest you listen to my wife. I got to go."

"Manny!" she screamed back into the phone. She cried. She tried to wipe her eyes before she entered the living room but couldn't control the emotions that ran down her face.

"You crying?" the woman said as she leaned off from the couch to grab the phone. "Honey, a little word of advice. Don't ever let a man who you haven't said 'I do' to make you cry." She turned to face, Cynthia. "Swallow up them tears and remember this day, remember all these emotions and use them when you're reading for your next part. If you're going to be an actress, you have to first understand that your emotions have to be controlled and not wasted. Use them only when necessary because they just might be the thing that gets you your next big break."

She grabbed her purse. "You're a pretty girl," she turned and said to Cynthia, "you're going to have to be more wise. Put your career first. If you really want it, in this industry it's going to have to come before babies, love, and marriage. You got to smarten up and toughen up if you're going to succeed in this industry." The woman stared back at Cynthia like she was a pathetic little thing. "Look, I don't usually do this but I'm feeling generous. If you decide to go through with the procedure, which I strongly advise you do, then I'll let you stay here an additional two weeks. Give you time to recover and find somewhere else to stay. But only two weeks. Good luck with your career and remember, put it first." She walked out the door.

"CENT, I'M MAKING a doctor's appointment for you two. Is Tuesday okay?" Daniel's mother asked.

"Appointment? We don't need a doctor. There's nothing wrong here," Daniel was insulted.

"No one is saying anything is wrong, son. It's just always good to seek a second opinion with these things. Especially from a professional. My doctor can give you some real tips. Not all that hocus pocus conception stuff you find off the internet."

Rodger hid his smile behind his dinner roll. Daniel gave Cynthia one of his *you did bad* looks.

"Don't get mad at Cent. I walked in on her doing one of the yoga downward dog things and asked her what it was about." Rodger laughed out loud.

"What are you laughing at, Rodger? Maybe you and your wife Katasha need to do the opposite. That one in her stomach is going to make three, son. You know anything over three is tacky." Rodger slumped down in a shameful slump. Daniel felt vindicated.

"Maybe a visit won't hurt," Daniel convinced himself, leaving Cynthia out of the decision.

"Could be something minor. Right, Denise?" Cynthia said to Daniel's second brother, Andrew's, wife.

"It's true," Denise said in a reassuring positive tone. "It almost took me and Andrew a year but after meeting with Dr. Michael, we were pregnant in a month. He's really good."

"And there're other alternatives, like In Vitro Fertilization," Rodger replied snidely.

"Gosh, no," Daniel's mother repeated disgusted. "They should call that In Desperation Fertilization. I mean, women go in there and pay thousands of dollars and next thing you know they're pregnant with a liter of babies. It's just unnatural and downright tacky," she vetoed the suggestion with a frown and sip of her wine.

"It just makes you think about that new abortion law they're trying to pass," Denise replied.

"The third trimester law? It's sick." Daniel's tone changed.

Cynthia started to shift in her seat. She hated when people brought up abortions. It was like someone opening a door, forcing her skeletons to fall out right at her feet.

"Well," Andrew replied. "I'm not a woman but if I was I would like to choose what I wanted to do with my body."

Cynthia smiled inwardly at his comment.

"What?" Daniel screamed. "Life is not a choice, it's a right. I think abortion is worse than murder. It's an abomination. He can kill a child?"

"Right or wrong, I'm just thankful I'm not a woman," Rodger interjected. "That seems to be a hard decision to live with. You know some religions say the spirit of the dead babies haunt the mother. That's eerie."

Rodger's comment made Cynthia so uneasy she almost dropped her wine glass. She avoided eye contact with all of them and remained quiet as she normally did when these conversations came up.

"I heard the baby is trapped in purgatory. Alone and scared," Katasha said. "I couldn't imagine my baby crying and no one being there to comfort him." She kissed her son on the forehead.

Cynthia nervously took a large gulp of wine from her glass. She felt like everyone at the table knew her secret and that they were talking about her. She could barely raise her eyes from the table.

"I heard that the mother has to face the baby in heaven. It's like the dead child decides if she gets in or not. Could you imagine facing the child you killed? What excuse is that mother going to have that's going to make up for their lost life?" Denise replied.

They all passed their judgment just like they did the dinner rolls. So cavalier and self-righteous.

"No one knows if all that is true or not," Andrew said.

"One thing for sure," their mother replied with a raised brow, "the pain. Studies show that those little innocent babies feel the pain of being pulled out of the womb. Imagine that," her voice lowered. "What a great deal of pain that must be for their little souls." She shook her head. "I don't want to have this conversation over dinner. I'm losing my appetite."

Cynthia was relieved the conversation was finally over. The topic of abortion was something she would rather read about not discuss. By the family's reaction to it, she knew that her secrets had to be ones that she died with.

It was Tuesday. The day Cynthia had been dreading. Cynthia didn't want to go to the doctor but she knew she couldn't avoid it. She feared that the doctor would poke at her secrets with his dipstick or bring them to light with his microscope, revealing them to a more than disapproving Daniel. The conversation Daniel sparked up during the ride to the office did nothing to ease her tension. It was a continuation of the family dinner conversation.

"I don't understand some women. Doesn't it just make you mad that they throw away the gift that we pray for?" Cynthia didn't respond. "You know my first wife, Patricia?" he said her name like it left a nasty taste in his mouth. He almost never mentioned his first wife, unless it was about the situation that caused their divorce; the situation Cynthia heard about more than once. Even more often now that they've been trying to conceive. "You know she killed our first child?" He opened the conversation with the same question that he always phrased like a statement. He was aware that Cynthia knew, but he always asked her. It was as if he were getting her permission to take the angry trip down memory lane. "I don't even know if it was boy or a girl. I wonder how she lives with herself?" he said under his breath.

"You know she told me she had a miscarriage?" Cynthia knew that too. "I actually felt for her, cared for her," he dragged his words, "I took off work for a damn week!" he yelled. "Helping her out of bed, nursing her back to health; she made me a part of her sickness. She made me an accessory to her crime." He victimized himself. "My colleagues and business associates all sympathized with me," he paused, "with us," he added. "Courtesy calls, flowers, apology cards. And mamma." He was silent. He stared out through the windshield, looking at blank space. "Mamma was hurt. Her first grandchild. My mamma treated that woman like a daughter."

Daniel shook his head. He mumbled under his breath. He was talking more to himself than he was to Cynthia. With each memory igniting more anger, he continued with his story. "I'll never forget that phone call. The follow-up call. Judy Tanner calling from the Choice Clinic to check on the status of her patient." His voice was high pitched as he imitated the woman's voice. "She had the nerve to sound peppy. Like she didn't have a care in the world. Like she didn't just assist my wife in killing our child and without my consent. When I confronted her, she didn't as much as blink. She showed no emotion, no remorse. It was like she wanted me to find out. Like she wanted to hurt me. She didn't deny it or admit it; she just stared at me like she was expecting me to read her mind. Well, I couldn't read her mind if I tried. We wanted to have that baby."

He was silent again. Normally, Cynthia would just let him vent. She didn't interrupt him or offer any negative feedback against Patricia to make him feel better. Mostly she just listened to every word. Trying to read in between the lines and find a clue as to why Patricia had done it. Experience told Cynthia that Patricia had a reason. Every woman did. So she asked him.

"Daniel, did you ever ask her why?"

"What? Why?" Daniel repeated like the question was absurd. "What could she tell me? Is there any reason for these kinds of things, Cynthia? I mean reasons beyond selfish needs and that ridiculous feminist empowerment bull." Cynthia didn't respond, although she knew there were several reasons why. Daniel was silent again but only briefly, then he responded, "Something about not being ready. I don't know. She has four kids now. Can you believe that? All four of those kids will never make up for the one she lost. Reasons?" he repeated. "There is no valid reason besides her being selfish."

Cynthia knew that there were reasons that couldn't be explained. Reasons that made sense even when the woman didn't understand them completely herself. But Daniel was right. Some of the reasons were selfish. But sometimes you had to be selfish in life. The third time Cynthia had an abortion she had decided to be selfish like Daniel's ex-wife. The timing wasn't right.

$\sim$

(The third reason why)

THE SOUND OF *the swish of paint brush against the concrete wall soothed the feel of the room. Cynthia loved watching him paint. It left a peaceful energy in the air. Cynthia stared at him from a distance as he attempted to achieve perfection through his brush. She didn't know how to tell him but knew that she had to. So she just blurted it out. "I'm pregnant."*

Her voice caught him off guard as he jumped, spilling more paint onto his black shirt. He stared back at Cynthia like she was the muse that inspired all his work. He attempted to wipe the paint from his face but only smeared more on. Cynthia felt that this made it easier for her. She really didn't want to see his reaction when she told him.

"A baby," he whispered, excited. He shook his head in disbelief then laughed out loud. "I dreamed of this moment, Cent. I…I dreamed it. The

piece I was working on couldn't come together, it had no meaning until now." He referred to his drawing. "At first I didn't understand but I get it now. This means everything is going to be okay." His eyes watered but no tears streamed down. He smiled wide while wearing a proud look on his face; like he had finally accomplished the success he couldn't find in his paintings. He stared at her stomach as if he was looking at his child. He extended his paint-crusted arm and rubbed her belly. "Man…my son is in there or daughter." He chuckled. "What a blessing. I can just see him now," he continued to rub, "or her," he said again. "We're going to move out here and get a bigger place and…"

Cynthia stopped him by removing his hand from her belly. She stepped back and slightly shook her head giving him a remorseful look. He lowered his brow while squinting his eye at Cynthia, as if he were trying to see into her mind.

"You're not excited?" he asked knowingly.

Cynthia didn't respond. She sighed before wiping the sweat from her forehead; she prepared herself for her response.

"I…I'm not excited," she said to him in a way that revealed her intentions.

He played dumb. "So, what does that mean? I mean lots of mothers are…you know… what are you trying to say, Cynthia?" He raised the tone of his voice.

"It's not the right time, Akell. You're on and off work and I'm…"

"You're going to punish me because of my work?" he cut her off. "Look, Cent, I'm an artist. I'm sorry if I'm not motivated by money but if it comes down to it I'll get a job, I'll sell a painting, I'll do what I have to do to take care of my child." He placed his hand on her stomach. He pleaded with her with his eyes. "Let's just give it a chance."

"My career is just taking off, Akell. It's not the time. I'm in a do-or-die time in my life. I got a call back…," she cracked a slight smile, "they want me for the rest of the season. That's the whole year, Akell and I'm in a take what I get stage. I don't have that type of pull yet that will allow them to write me in as pregnant woman."

"A do-or-die situation, huh? So you choose death." His tone was cold.

"You don't understand," Cynthia responded.

"Don't expect me to. God doesn't make mistakes and He has a better sense of timing than all of us."

"Now you're getting religious on me?" Cynthia said disgusted.

"It's more than religion. It's morality; it's fucking with the universe; it's my child, Cent. It's not an old purse, or a tube of lipstick you can just throw out. It's me and it's you and your mother and my mother and my father and your fa..."

"I'm not trying to hear this poetic shit because this is the real world, Akell. I live in the real world and you live somewhere else," she waved her arms in the air. "In the real world, we sometimes are faced with difficult choices and we make difficult decisions. This is my decision."

"So what am I? I can't make this decision?" he yelled.

"This decision doesn't affect you like it affects me," Cynthia defended her choice.

"Just have the baby and give it to me," he bargained with her. "You don't have to see it, I won't bother you, you can..."

"STOP!" she screamed. "It's not that easy. I can't just have this baby, Akell. I just can't. I've worked so hard for this and I'm finally at the point where I can get there. It's right here in my hand, Akell," she held her hand. "All I have to do is grab it."

"What's in your belly outweighs anything you can ever obtain in your hand." He placed his hands on his face and moved them upward, stopping at his hair line. He pushed back his locks and lowered his head to the ground like he was saying a silent prayer. He exhaled and looked up at Cynthia. He clasped his hands together in a praying gesture, and rested it on his nose. Then he asked in a low serious tone, "Are you going to kill our child?"

Cynthia didn't respond, so he asked again, this time louder. "Are... you...going...to...kill...our child!" Still no response from the teary eyed Cynthia. He hit the wall. "Are you? Are you?" he raged.

"Yes!" she screamed back. "But I'm no murderer. Don't put that on me. I'm not a murderer," she said in between sobs.

"You're the worst kind of murderer. A child killer. A premeditated child killer. Selfish, self-centered," he said the words like they left a nasty taste in his mouth. "Corrupt," he said closer to Cynthia's face. His eyes were squinted into an evil stare. "You're disgusting. You disgust me."

"Don't," Cynthia pleaded. She reached out to touch his face but he jumped away from her touch like her evil was contagious. "Don't touch me with those bloody hands." He stepped away from her. "Why did you even tell me, Cent?"

"I thought you deserved to know," her voice cracked.

"I deserved to know?" he whispered loudly, surprised by her response. "You think I deserve to know this? I deserved to know that you're going to suck our child out and let some machine chop his little body up. I deserve to know that?" He punched the wall again, this time his fist went through it. Cynthia shirked. "What man deserves to know that? What man deserves to live the rest of his life knowing that he has a dead child he'll never get to meet because the mother thought it wasn't the right time? Huh? Cent. What man deserves to know that! You wanted to torture me, huh. Is that it?" He punched the wall again. "What did I do to deserve this? I...I loved you too much, I'm too poor, I'm not famous enough, what?" he began to cry.

"I'm sorry, Akell. I'm sorry." She begged for his understanding more than his forgiveness.

He sniffed up his tears and wiped his face. After clearing his throat, he replied, "You're wrong, Cynthia. Wrong in so many ways."

"I have to live with this too."

"You deserve to live with this; I don't." He chuckled sarcastically. "Oh, and you better believe you're going to live with this. Every day of every second of your life, you're going to remember this mistake. You're going to regret it. Don't forget that the earth is round. It may take years, but sooner or later the world is going to spin in your direction, and you're going to remember this day and regret it."

He was right.

DANIEL PARKED THE car. Before pulling the key out the ignition, he straightened out the wrinkles of his grimacing face and turned to Cynthia. "I'm sorry. I shouldn't be charging up all these negative energy before we go to meet the doctor. Everything is going to be alright, honey. I promise." He patted Cynthia on the knee.

Five minutes later, Cynthia was dressed in a hospital gown. She laid on her back on an exam table. The walls were plastered with posters of fat white babies and pregnant women holding their perfectly round bellies. The women smiled. They seemed to be smiling at Cynthia; their smiles looked condescending.

"Okay, place your feet here," the doctor said and turned the stirrups. She placed her feet in the straps and spread her legs while the doctor aimed a warm light in between her legs before rolling in closer with his chair. Cynthia felt humiliated. The doctor didn't bother to tell her what he was looking for and she didn't bother to ask him. They both already knew though. Lying on that metal table with her feet strapped in and her knees shaking was too familiar. It could have all been over if she would have had the courage to tell him the truth; she didn't have courage.

They were back in the waiting room. Cynthia was both relieved and terrified that the test was over.

"How do you feel?" Daniel asked.

Cynthia shrugged, then smiled.

"I feel positive too. Maybe, he'll prescribe you some vitamins or something. I'm sure he'll tell me to stop eating red meat and drinking red wine." Daniel laughed nervously. "It's great that he's giving us the results today. You know that's not normal. It's good being my mother's child, huh?" Cynthia nodded. She tried to hide her anxieties. She flipped through a magazine, but everything in the magazine, the office, and on the walls intensified her anxiety.

"The doctor will see you now" a voice from the receptionist window said out.

Daniel jumped, anxious, and held out his hand for Cynthia to grab. Cynthia wiped the sweat from her palms onto her dress and grabbed

Daniel's hand. He squeezed her hand to comfort her but it only made her feel uncomfortable.

Cynthia and Daniel faced the doctor. Daniel's eyes were filled with hope. Like the doctor was the creator himself. The doctor looked over his notes. Cynthia tried to read his face. Maybe it can give her a heads up on what he was about to say, give her time to prepare herself but his face showed no hint of emotion.

"Who should I start with?" the doctor asked without looking up from his notes.

"Doesn't matter. Me, her," Daniel joked uneasily. "I guess her," he confirmed. "Start with my wife, start with my wife."

"Now, I'm going to have to ask some very personal questions, so I don't want any of you getting offended."

"Okay," Daniel answered for both of them.

"How long have you and your wife been trying to conceive?"

"About six months now, right?" he looked to Cynthia. She answered with a smile and a nod.

"Cynthia, are you on any birth control?"

"Birth control?" Daniel replied. "Doctor, we just told you that we're trying to conceive."

"Daniel, again. I have to ask these questions in order to give you a proper analysis."

"No," Cynthia answered.

"Have you ever been on any kind of birth control other than condoms?"

"No," she replied again.

"Have you ever been diagnosed with a sexually transmitted disease?"

Daniel sighed.

Cynthia answered no again.

"Have you ever had an abortion?"

Cynthia hesitated. The question she had been waiting on, the question she had been dreading. She didn't know how to respond. It was a close end question; no opening to list her three reasons why. Daniel didn't roll his eyes at this question. He didn't suck his teeth or annoyingly tap his foot. He watched and waited on the response. She wished she could ask the doctor to rephrase the question. Rephrase it in a way that she didn't appear to be the monster Daniel thought his first wife was.

Cynthia didn't want the answer to the question to be the reason for their problems. Her past was supposed to be her past. Hidden and almost non-existent. She stared down at her feet, then up at the wall behind the doctor. She wasn't ready to look him in the eye. She could feel Daniel staring at her, growing more nervous by her delayed response by the second. Cynthia turned to face Daniel. If time could freeze for one minute, then she would have time to explain but it wasn't an explanation they were waiting for, it was an answer.

"Yes," she answered. Her voice cracked and her eyes dropped.

Daniel didn't blink. She knew he was embarrassed. The doctor didn't flinch. The emotion in his face didn't change one bit, this made it a little easier but Daniel's consistent look made it worse. Still no noise, no shifting in his seat; no reaction to what she said at all.

"How many?" the doctor continued.

Cynthia didn't understand why that mattered at this point but she answered any way.

"Three," Cynthia answered. She turned to look at Daniel. He looked as though he had checked out; only the shell of him stared back at her.

"Okay, well I saw scarring and bruising in certain areas during my examination. The multiple abortions may be the cause but then again, they may not be."

Multiple abortions. The doctor using the word multiple made her feel like a serial killer.

"Can she conceive?" Daniel finally spoke. His tone was stern but soft. However, under it, she held a little hope.

The doctor answered with his eyes first; finally, the heads-up Cynthia had been waiting for. Then he spoke, "No."

"Thank you, doctor," Daniel stood up to shake his hand; he shook the doctor's hand like he was sealing a business deal. Daniel kept his cool.

"Do you want to hear your results?" the doctor asked Daniel.

Daniel looked confused. He looked down at Cynthia who was still sitting in the chair and then back at the doctor.

"The results of your testing. I think you should have a seat sir," the doctor encouraged Daniel.

Hesitantly, he sat back down.

"Your sperm count is abnormally low. It's my professional opinion that you can't conceive either," he said to Daniel with a straight face.

Instantly, Cynthia felt relieved. The burden was taken off of her. Daniel turned to her for emotional support and she grabbed his hand.

"Plenty of couples in your situation consider adoption. You can still be parents."

"Adoption," Daniel said the words like it was a death sentence. "No, you have to run your test again, doc." Daniel was in denial. "My first wife conceived and.."

Then a light bulb went off in his head. Now he knew the reason she had an abortion. It wasn't his baby. Daniel jumped up and straightened his shoulder. He cleared his throat and held out his hand for the doctor to shake.

"Thank you, doctor," Daniel said with a smile. "Honey, are you ready to go?" He held out his hand for Cynthia to grab.

On the way out the door, he turned to Cynthia and said, "We will get a second opinion. Don't worry, babe, we just have to be patient."

The End

The Perfect Picture

NIGEL SWIVELED THE brush against the canvas with the snap of his wrist attempting to achieve perfection that seemed unattainable. Squinting his marble shaped eyes while leaning in closer to the canvas, Nigel was ready to give up for the day. He had locked himself in the room and stayed there for almost three hours. Dried up patches of paint covered most of his face with the exception of the tiny streaks of skin that peeked out near his temples. Beads of sweat created a cleared path for his skin to show. The fumes from the paint began to make their way through his nostrils causing him to feel disoriented, yet this feeling was nothing compared to the harsh reality that patiently waited outside the door. His painting room had become his escape as he made his own little world with all his emotions and thoughts controlled by what he smeared on the canvas.

As soon as Nigel stepped his foot outside the room, he was greeted by an overwhelming flood of emotion. Most of it was heartbreak but the other half was loneliness and fear. These emotions haunted his house. They hid in every corner, catching him off guard and attacking him when he least expected it. Trying to ignore the emotions that weighed down his spirit like an anchor and attached itself to his soul, Nigel took a deep breath and blew at air. He always tried that method first but it never worked. So he did the other one thing besides painting that gave him instant relief. He headed towards the refrigerator in pursuit of his whiskey, his self-prescribed medication. It was the quickest way for him to ease the pain. Leaning over the refrigerator and pulling out the bottle, Nigel's eyes landed on the small magnetic calendar that clasped onto the refrigerator. Mouthing out the date of March 13, the image of her almond shaped, auburn colored eyes and two fluffy powder puffs flashed through his mind causing a pain to jolt through his body, striking him like lighting. The memory of his daughter, Jonah, cracked and echoed like thunder. An emotional storm was coming. Jonah would have been seven years old today. Every year on her birthday, he was tortured by the constant reminder of her absence. He instantly remembered his daughter's sweet voice and gentle spirit.

"He's got the whole world in his hand…he's got the whole world in his hand," Jonah sang. "Daddy God must really be big if He got the whole world in his hand," Jonah said while spreading out her arms.

"Yep J, He's really big."

"But not too big so that he doesn't see us," she said innocently.

Nigel often wondered if Jonah ever belonged to him. Whenever he wrapped his arms around her tiny body, he felt as if she were slipping away; no hug was ever long enough.

Even as a baby he had always gotten the sense that she had been here before. She had a way of looking straight through people as if she could see the real them. The part that God sees. The good parts. Her curious mind seemed to create a million questions, yet she always seemed to know the answer.

"Daddy, where do birds go when they fly?"

"Um….

"They fly underneath heaven with the angels," she quickly replied like God himself whispered the answer in her ear.

Her fascination with birds led them to several different parks where they sat in silence while she watched with an analytical eye as the birds interacted with one another in the air. Nigel dedicated several hours of work painting her pictures of birds flying against the wind. No picture ever seemed perfect enough, so he would get to work on a new one before the paint had time to dry on the last.

"Daddy, why do you give me so many pictures?" Jonah asked maturely.

"Because, I'm trying to get it just right for you, baby. I want it to be perfect."

"But daddy there's no such thing as perfect." she replied with her hands on her hip and brow raised. "Only in heaven, daddy. Only heaven is perfect," she informed Nigel. "You'll see when you get there."

~

THE MEMORY OF his daughter was too painful. Nigel wrapped his lips around the bottle and swallowed in large gulps in attempts to drown the pain that threatened to overwhelm him. After hearing the faint sound of footsteps creaking against the wooden floor, Nigel immediately buried the bottle of whiskey deep into the refrigerator with the same pace a fourteen-year-old would use in the surprise presence of their parents. With it being Jonah's birthday, he knew that his wife, Asia, would be trying extra hard to hide her pain. Nigel hated the way she mourned their daughter's death. He had seen her cry two times and that wasn't enough for him. Once at the hospital and the other at the funeral. After that, it was as if her tears had evaporated from the fuming heat of her anger. She instantly took on the role that everyone expected him to play, she appeared to be the strong one. But Nigel just saw her as cold. The only warmth he got from her came from the heat of her anger. She blamed him for it all. That was the worst part of it.

Nigel felt like he had taken the place of the child in her life. She constantly nagged him about everything she could and controlled his every move. Like a teenager, Nigel would grunt obscenities under his breath while taking deep breaths to balance his emotions. She controlled every aspect of their life, even their love making. Every blue moon she would allow him to be with her by initiating her nonverbal gesture of her knee slightly pressing against his back. He knew that meant she was allowing sex for the night but she was too prideful and broken to ask for it. She didn't want Nigel to think she needed anything from him, so she gave him space to initiate the sex and that way she could control if it happened or not. Their lovemaking was more of a robotic act than an intimate moment. Asia dictated where he could touch her and whenever his hands ventured off into a restricted area of her body, a part that would evoke too much pleasure, Asia would abort the mission by pushing his weight off her body before moving over to her designated spot on the edge of the bed, away from Nigel.

Normally, they slept in the same queen-sized bed, but with two separate blankets. Whenever Nigel's toe would mistakenly touch the tip of her toe, she would instantly scoot her body further to the end of the bed with half of her hip dangling off the edge. The bed wasn't big enough for the both of them and Asia made it very clear that she didn't want him touching her so most nights Nigel slept on the couch or in his studio.

He watched his wife out of the corner of his eye, hoping that today would be one of those silent days where she treated him like he didn't exist, but that was only wishful thinking.

"Is that alcohol I smell?" Asia asked disapprovingly to Nigel's back while twirling her nose in a sniffing motion.

"Nope," Nigel said while closing the refrigerator.

"Well I hope not because I'm not peeling your drunk carcass off the couch. Tonight you're just going to freeze," she said without ever making eye contact.

Nigel watched her as she fumbled through the mail and waited for her next shot at him. Observing the paper she held in her hand, Asia's eyes widened and lips twisted as she became distracted by a text notification from the bank.

"Nigel, what did you spend 75 dollars on today? I mean, 75 dollars in one day? Nigel, you know money doesn't grow on trees and it surely doesn't grow on them canvases you have collecting dust in that back room. I have to go out and work ten hour shifts to get money, Nigel," Her head tilted in the same disapproving manner one would use with a ten-year-old child.

"I just bought a brush and grabbed some lunch while I was out."

"I thought we agreed on you having lunch at home. That's why I bought the sandwich meat, and what's wrong with the brushes you got? Buying a new brush isn't going to get you your perfect picture," she yelled before slamming the bank statement onto the counter. "I'll add money tree to my list, Nigel. I'm everything else for you, so I might as well be your damn money tree, too."

Nigel leaned against the refrigerator with his eyes lowered to the ground. He had become numb to her treatment. He even convinced himself that he deserved it. The constant insults and bickering had already done their assigned damage and now Nigel was just left with the after effects. He hadn't sold a painting in almost a year and alcohol was beginning to take the place of his career and marriage. The whiskey burned out all of his disappointment, helping him to digest the reality of what his life had become. He remembered a time when he used to think his wife was the sweetest woman he had ever met. Her charismatic personality always attracted people to her in droves and her laugh was contagious. She used to watch him with innocent eyes, naïve to the pain of love and loss. Back then she had faith.

The day he met Asia she was doing cartwheels across a football field. It was the perfect place for Nigel to paint and it was where Asia coached the peewee cheerleading team. Nigel was immediately captivated by her beauty. It was as if with every flip she brought more life to the dull field of dry yellow grass. It was then that he decided to secretly paint her portrait. When he finished, Asia boldly walked up to him like she knew he had something for her.

~୨

"*WANNA FLIP?*" ASIA *asked Nigel.*

"No…No, I can't flip," Nigel answered bashfully.

"Everybody can flip," Asia joked.

"I'm not a flipper."

"We all are." She giggled before raising her arms and curving her body towards the wind. Nigel watched her small framed body bounce off the ground. The wind blew her naturally kinked hair in front of her almond shaped eyes, temporarily blinding her and throwing her off balance. She tumbled head first into the grass. Nigel ran to her aid, but when he got to her, she was lying in the grass with the sun enhancing the glow of her golden brown complexion and her mouth stuffed full of laughter. The unique chirps that poured out of her mouth caused Nigel to laugh as well.

"Are you okay?"

He buried his knee into the moist grass.

"You should really try flipping sometime." She chuckled. Asia continued to roll around in the grass full of energy. Nigel stared at her twisting body as the wind blew a wave of chemistry their way. As the rays of the sun highlighted her beauty, Nigel thought to himself that Asia was the perfect picture.

NIGEL TIP-TOED OUT of the kitchen sticking his neck out and examining the corners of the house, making sure that there was no sign of Asia. When he saw the coast was clear, he headed towards their bedroom in pursuit of her purse where she had her sleeping pills stuffed deep into the bottom; it was the only way he could get through the night. Nigel's dreams were the one place where he could see Jonah. He continued to have the same dream almost every night. They would always be at the park.

He would hear the trail of her voice giggling in the wind and follow the sound. Then there in a field of grass would be Jonah standing under the blinding rays of the sun surrounded by hundreds of birds and motioning with her tiny finger for him to come closer. But the closer he got to her, the further away she seemed. Some nights he would get close enough to reach out and grab her, but whenever he did, she would leap off the ground and fly away with the birds, disappearing deep into the clouds.

Whenever he had this dream he would wake up with the same tight feeling of his chest sinking down into his stomach. Some nights he didn't want to get up and hated Asia for nudging him with the pointed edge of her elbow, breaking the little time he had with Jonah. Tonight he had planned to take enough pills so that not even a bomb would distract him from his mission of reaching his daughter in his dream. While tuning into the sounds of the house to make sure Asia wouldn't catch him in her purse, Nigel dug through all the items in pursuit of the pills. Reaching deep into the bag he felt the rigidness of the bottle's top on the tip of his fingers and pulled it from her purse along with a folded piece of paper that he mistakenly grabbed. Usually Nigel wasn't the type to invade the privacy of her purse, but there was something about the folded paper that flirted with his curiosity.

Nigel carefully opened the paper and his eyes immediately landed on the words, *pregnancy termination.* The familiar feeling of his heart being placed on a bungee strap and plunged downward to a never ending nowhere, overwhelmed his body while he struggled to keep the strength in his legs. The agonizing pain he felt was quickly replaced by anger as he clutched the paper in his hand.

"What the hell are you doing in my purse?" Asia yelled.

Asia thought she caught him but really, he caught her. Nigel held up the letter so that she could see it and watched Asia's posture change as her shoulders slumped down while her eyes searched the wood floor, avoiding eye contact.

"What is this?" he whispered loudly. Asia's mood shifted as she folded her arms across her chest while straightening out the slouch in her back. She stared straight into Nigel's bulging eyes.

"Can't you read?" Asia stared back at Nigel with a cold gaze.

Nigel buried his nails deep into the palms of his hand while tightening his jaw with the grinding of his teeth. The lines of his forehead thickened making him appear older while the pulse in his neck began to throb. He was beyond angry.

"You killed my child?"

"Well, that makes us even," Asia said with a straight face like she actually believed her rhetoric.

Before Nigel knew it, he had raised his right hand, striking Asia's cheek. The feel of Asia's skin against his hand left him shocked, causing him to apologize before her face could feel the sting.

"What are you sorry for? Nothing can hurt me anymore, Nigel," Asia didn't flinch. "You think that hurt? You don't know pain."

"Why did you do it Asia? It was our child, just like Jon…"

"Don't you dare say her name," she raised her index finger so that it brushed the tip of Nigel's nose. "It would have been nothing like Jonah. No one can ever take her place."

She pounded on his chest with a balled fist. The pain of this discovery was nothing compared to the night they lost Jonah.

ALTHOUGH THE SKY *lit up with streaks of electrifying blue and echoed with large cracks of thunder, Jonah continued to sing her favorite Sunday school song unmoved by the threat of the storm. They were on their way home from a weekend at the mountains. They went there every other month to spend quality time as a family, away from the chaos of the city. It was a three hour drive back home and Nigel had decided to drive through the storm, against Asia's better judgment.*

"Nigel, what's one day? It's getting kind of bad out here."

"We've driven through worse. Besides, you know I have that show to get ready for. I can't miss it, honey. Jonah you're not scared, are you?"

"No, I'm not scared for me. But I'm scared for you," she said innocently then quickly continued on with her song.

Nigel stretched his neck out as close as he could to the windshield, attempting to see the dark road. "Nigel, let's just go back, honey. The show can wait. Besides, I wouldn't mind having you for an extra day or two."

Nigel ignored his wife's request and continued to squint his eyes in an attempt to see past the rain. After five miles of battling the storm, they had finally gotten far enough so that only drizzles of rain sprinkled onto the car.

"See, told you I was going to get us through it," Nigel complimented himself.

"Look daddy, reindeers," Jonah pointed out towards the woods.

"Ooh," Nigel honked his horn. "They need to go back to Santa."

Before Nigel could blink, he was slamming on his breaks and swerving the wheel towards the right of the road attempting to get away from the deer that stood, unmoved, in front of their car. The slickness from the rain caused the wheels to spin out of control hitting a curb and then blowing out his back tire. Nigel turned the wheel left, right, and then back towards the left again striving to regain control over the car, but it was too late. He felt the car going in the direction of a steep hill, off the side of the road. The car dipped, plunging down the hill full speed with tree branches and dirt scraping and cracking the windshield. All Nigel could think of was his daughter. After the car smashed into a tree, shattering the glass into tiny pieces and ejecting him from his seat belt, he didn't have to wonder because he had already known she was gone. The impact of the tree forced the life out of her tiny, four-year-old body. When she left, Nigel had willingly given his spirit to his daughter and still felt that it wasn't enough to offer, but his wife had been robbed of her spirit and left with nothing but an empty hollowness from buried pain.

NIGEL STEPPED BACK from her flying arms battling with her fist in an attempt to restrain her punches. He locked on to both her wrists, forcing her back into the wall.

"You bitch…you murdering bitch. You just gave me a reason to leave. After all these years, I've been trying to find a reason to leave you and start my life over. I dream about leaving you. You killed our daughter just as much as I did and you don't even know it. You did worse, Asia. You killed the memory of her. I can't even say her name around you and I'm tired of hiding the fact that I miss her while tip-toeing around your selfish mood swings. I have a better relationship with a bottle than I have with you. I can't take it anymore. You killed the last chance of us ever having anything again. Do you really hate life so much that you have to destroy anything that resembles it? I gave enough of my life to you. Tonight, I'm taking it back."

Nigel observed Asia's body as it slid down the wall in slow motion. Her eyes were so saturated with tears that Nigel couldn't see her pupils. While groaning with anger and pain, she began to pull at her hair as if the pain from it would keep her from feeling the emotions she locked in her heart. Nigel didn't cater to his wife's fit. For the first time in their marriage, he had the last word.

He rushed to their bedroom and began stuffing items into a garbage bag. The heavier the garbage bag got, the less weight he felt like he was carrying. He had one last stop to make before turning the door knob of his future. He walked into his art room and observed the mess. Half-finished portraits of birds lay scattered on the floor accompanied by empty whiskey bottles. He looked at his less than perfect pictures and at that moment wondered what he was really trying to achieve.

The sound of his daughter's voice saying "there's no such thing as the perfect picture" echoed through his mind, causing him to fall to his knees. Overwhelmed by the memory of their life before the accident, he knew that it was his turn to flip. He buried his face into the dust that laced the wood floor and began to pound against the floor boards while moaning sorrowful screams.

Nigel glimpsed over at his portrait of a bird soaring off into the wind. He immediately began to analyze the uneven lining of the bird's wings and the smudges that caked across the clouds. Underneath the pile of dust was the portrait he painted of his wife flipping in the field. The picture reminded him of everything that he was missing. Her smile, her laugh, her attractive energy, and, most of all, her love. The same love that inspired him to pursue his career as an artist. The same love he thought would never die. The same love that created the purest love of all. Their daughter, Jonah. It was then that he realized that he couldn't paint his perfect picture on the canvas. This was the picture he had to use his mind to create.

He began to grab all the pictures, with the exception of his wife's, from the ground, cracking them under his knee before stomping on top of them. Destroying these pictures was the closest Nigel had gotten to moving on. With all the years he'd spent trying to reach his daughter through his dream, Nigel finally recognized that it wasn't his daughter he was reaching for but his wife. The best parts of her that died in the crash with their daughter. With her portrait in hand, he raced to the bedroom to confront her. He was going to show her the picture, hoping that it would help her remember their love. When he got to the bedroom, she wasn't there. "Asia," he called out as he began to search the rooms in the house. When he got to the bathroom, the sight of his wife made his body weak. The portrait slipped from his hand and cracked onto the floor. He rushed to the phone to call for help before returning back to the bathroom.

Nigel stared down at Asia's quivering body feeling both relief and remorse at the same time. Her hair sat in a mangled knot at the top of her head while her oversized t-shirt drooped off her slender shoulder, revealing her chest as it sunk in and out with every shallow breath. He watched her as she clutched her left wrist with her right hand. Blood streamed out between her fingers forming neat puddles of red as it dripped elegantly onto the white tiled floor. Choking on her tears, large drops of saliva hung off her bottom lip while she mumbled the word "sorry" under her breath although her squinted eyes and lowered brow told a different story. Asia was sad but also angry. She couldn't handle being blamed for her daughter's death.

Nigel didn't recognize the woman whose body was stuffed between the tub and toilet. This was a side of her that he never knew existed. Although it was a gruesome sight to witness, he felt relieved because now he knew she, too, could feel. He needed to see this just to know that he wasn't alone. Nigel stood in the doorway calculating his next move while approaching his wife with caution. He was careful. He kept his eyes on the razor and she kept her eyes on him. Asia didn't want Nigel to touch her. The closer he got to her the more she pressed her body against the wall. He carefully extended his hand in front of her and made a grabbing motion but Asia pulled the razor out of the puddle of blood and began to slice at the small space that separated her and Nigel. With sprinkles of blood flying in the air, Nigel tried his best to avoid contact with the blade. Not accurately timing the reach of his hand with the swing of the blade, his wife embedded the razor deep into the palm of his hand ripping away the flesh. The sharp prick of the razor caused Nigel to fall back. The wall caught his weight before his body slowly slid down to the floor. He stared back at his wife and instantly began to mourn her. Through that mourning, he realized how much he still loved her. Even in her worst state, through the blood and tears, Nigel was able to see remnants of the woman she used to be. He was able to see the human in her. The part of her that could feel.

They had buried what was left of their marriage with their daughter. Their marriage was left to suffocate and rot in a coffin, six feet under the earth where it could not be reached without both of them digging. Though he promised to stay with her through sickness and health, Nigel felt as though being with her was emotional suicide. Before she put a knife to her wrist, she managed to take away the last meaningful feeling he had left. A second chance at life. Another child. He knew that no one could ever replace Jonah but the child she aborted would heal them both, in a way, their unborn was Jonah. Nigel stared back at his wife before pulling himself up from the floor. He wrapped his hand up a towel and took deep breaths to control the pain.

"Asia, I love you." Nigel kept his eyes fixed on his wife. "I'm not going anywhere," he admitted.

Asia's head had become too heavy for her neck to support. She swayed in and of consciousness. Nigel grabbed a towel from the hamper and wrapped it around her saturated wrist before scooting her body off the ground. He gently kissed her forehead before carrying her out into the living room. "I love you too, Nigel. I'm sorry," she whispered faintly. Before Nigel could lay her down on the couch, the paramedics were bursting through door. The medics hovered over his wife's body, trying their best to save her life. Nigel watched and prayed. For the first time since Jonah's death, he was able to see Jonah through his wife. Tears flowed down his cheeks in neat streams as he stood motionless.

Nigel prayed to himself in silence in the hospital's waiting room. He couldn't lose his wife and his second child on the day of Jonah's birthday. It was all too much for him to bear.

"Sir, are you the husband?" Nigel nodded and jumped up. "Did you know that your wife is expecting?" Nigel's eyes widened as he stared at the doctor in shock. She didn't kill the baby.

"Expecting?" he repeated. "No, I didn't know," Nigel said through a hidden smile.

"Yep, about six weeks in. The baby is fine. After we stabilize your wife, she should be fine too. They're going to make it," the doctor said.

Emergency doors opened and a bird flew in, catching the doctor off guard. She screamed, but it didn't startle Nigel. He knew it was a sign. A sign from Jonah. Nigel exhaled through a smile while mouthing the words, *thank you*, to Jonah. All those years he spent trying to create the perfect picture for her, Jonah returned the favor and gave him his perfect picture. Finally, Nigel was at peace.

The End

MORE BOOKS BY THIS AUTHOR

THE BADD WIVES SERIES

ALL THREE TITLES AVAILABLE ON AMAZON

BADD WIVES (BOOK 1)

CONFESSIONS OF A BADD WIFE (BOOK 2)

BADD BLOOD (BOOK 3)

PLEASE LEAVE A REVIEW

If you enjoyed this book, please leave a review and/or share this story.

GoodReads, Amazon and Bookbub

SUBSCRIBE TO MY NEWSLETTER

Want to stay in touch? Subscribe to my newsletter to receive notifications for free books, new releases and other giveaways.

LET'S KEEP IN TOUCH

FOLLOW ME:
Facebook @ThisWritersLife
Instagram @AuthorZee.W.
Email authorzee.w@gmail.com

www.ingramcontent.com/pod-product-compliance
Lightning Source LLC
Chambersburg PA
CBHW07075118O626
46818CB00007B/3079